KISSING KENDALL

A GONE WILD NOVEL

KATEE ROBERT

TRINKETS AND TALES LLC

ALSO BY KATEE ROBERT

GONE WILD SERIES

Kissing Kendall by Katee Robert

Gaming Grace by Piper J Drake

Attraction Aubrey by Avery Flynn

Beguiling Benjamin by Robin Covington

Loving Liv by Stacey Kennedy

CONTENT WARNING

This book contains an unexpected death in the family, and may be triggering for some readers.

CHAPTER 1

*K*endall Barnes realized she'd made a terrible mistake the second she saw the pseudo-orgy going on by the pool. Did it even count as an orgy if they still had their clothes on and the ship hadn't left New York? She wasn't sure, but her face flamed at the way the group of five —*five?*—people surged and rolled as they made out and ground on each other. She couldn't be sure, but she was pretty sure that guy had his hand down that girl's pants and—

She turned away.

This was wrong.

This was very, very wrong.

"Kendall, those people are—"

"I know," she grabbed Grace and steered her away from the scene behind them. She'd known booking this cruise was a risk. Everyone knew cruises were a risk, what with so many people sandwiched in a relatively small space. But Kendall had been prepared to battle norovirus or seasickness or pirates. She was *not* prepared to deal with people getting

1

to third base right there on the deck. They hadn't even left port yet!

Their other three friends had already had their rooms assigned, but she and Grace were left to wander a little bit before theirs were ready. She looked around and finally landed on one of the cruise employees in their official-looking white uniform. "We'll just report them."

"*Report* them?"

She didn't give Grace a chance to argue, towing her along and dodging people streaming onto the ship. The guy in white gave them a professional smile as they approached, his dark skin gleaming in the bright sunlight. "How can I help you?"

Kendall made a vague motion over her shoulder. "Those people…"

The man leaned a little and smiled. "They're getting the party started early, it seems."

"Party?" She cleared her throat, well aware that her skin had to be crimson at this point judging by the heat in her cheeks. "Don't you think it's a little inappropriate for them to be… fornicating… on the deck when this is supposed to be a nice relaxing cruise?"

His dark brows rose. "Ma'am, that is the *least* of what you'll see over the next eight days on the party cruise."

Did he just…

He did.

She didn't realize she was tightening her grip on Grace's arm until her friend grabbed Kendall's wrist and forced her to let go. Kendall cleared her throat again, striving for calm that she could feel slipping through her fingers. "I'm sorry, I thought you said party cruise, but that can't possibly be right because I booked a *low-key relaxing cruise.*"

His smile went sympathetic. "One of your friends put this

together, right? They must have thought it would be a great surprise. That happens from time to time."

She heard his words, but they still made no sense. Kendall didn't make mistakes. When she put together the perfect plan to reconnect with her old college friends, she'd worked with a travel agent to organize it down to the smallest detail. She had very specifically *not* booked a party cruise. She was not the kind of person who booked a party cruise. If anyone, that was her little sister's thing. In fact, she was pretty sure Marley went on one last year.

She shook her head. "There's been a mistake."

"Kendall."

She turned to look at Grace. Her friend didn't look like she was seconds from the panic attack Kendall could feel bubbling up in her chest. Grace's dark eyes narrowed and she took Kendall's shoulders. "Breathe."

"I am breathing."

"You're two seconds from freaking out."

She wasn't wrong. Kendall closed her eyes and concentrated on breathing. Without the sight of the orgy-in-waiting, she could almost pretend they were on the right cruise. Almost. "We have to get off this boat."

"Kendall, that's impossible."

She opened her eyes. "Nothing's impossible. You just have to speak to the right people."

Grace sighed. "Let's walk through it logically. Even if we could get to the others in time and convince them to leave the ship, our trip is paid for. We've all taken this exact block of time off work. We're *here*. The only thing that makes sense is to continue the vacation as planned."

As planned. Two little words to underscore how thoroughly she'd messed up. Kendall wrapped her arms around herself and tried to ignore the pressure building in her chest. "I'm sorry. I'm so sorry. The whole trip is ruined."

"The trip hasn't even started yet," Grace's wry tone snapped her out of it.

What was she thinking? This couldn't possibly be worse than any other disaster she'd successfully navigated. She just needed to find the right angle and drag the rest of them along with her. Yes, she couldn't have possibly anticipated a *party* cruise in place of the nice sedate one planned, but she hadn't anticipated that her boss would run off with the front desk manager last year, either. She'd handled that crisis, and she'd handle this one too.

Simple.

This time, when she inhaled, it didn't snag in her chest. "You're right."

"I know."

Kendall managed a smile. "Let's get our rooms situated and then we'll figure out the rest."

"Figure out the rest," Grace repeated, giving her a look like she was a tiger in a cage. "You know you're on vacation, correct?"

"You're one to talk." She didn't comment on Grace's aversion to vacation wear, which really translated into an aversion to wearing *shorts*. It didn't make much difference now, while it was still cold and windy and they were too far north for anything resembling *warm*, but Grace wouldn't change her mind once the sticky heat set in. She'd just suffer in silence as if that made any kind of sense. Then again, they all had their quirks. "The only reason you agreed to this is because your CEO forced you to."

Grace opened her mouth, seemed to reconsider, and closed it. "Let's find our rooms."

"Checkmate." Kendall laughed, but it came out half-hearted. One of the cruise people called Grace's name and she waved her off. "Go get your room and warm up. I'll see you in a little bit when we meet for drinks." She *needed* a drink after this spectacular failure. She managed to keep her smile in place until Grace disappeared into the crowd, and then Kendall let her shoulders slump.

She should have known this would go sideways before the cruise ship even departed. If there was one law she ascribed to above all others, it was Murphy's. Anything that could go wrong, did. Every. Single. Time. It started with the death of her parents when she was nine, and it hadn't let up in the sixteen years since. Not once. She'd thought this trip would be the exception, the turning point she so desperately needed.

She really should have known better.

A sensation swept over her, stalling her before she could start pacing. Someone was watching her, their attention a weight she could feel as surely as she felt the cold nipping at her skin. She looked around slowly, telling herself this was silly even as she did. It didn't matter if someone was watching her. This was a freaking singles party cruise; no doubt people would look at her and assume she wanted in on the activities. They'd be wrong, of course. Kendall didn't do wild, and she sure as hell didn't hook up. With her long-running bad luck, it'd end even worse than her handful of relationships had over the years. She shuddered at the thought.

Her shudder turned into something else altogether when she met blue eyes across the deck. The man they belonged to leaned against the railing, looking particularly unaffected in his weathered jeans and leather jacket. His dark hair barely ruffled in the wind, and his square jaw looked sharp enough to cut herself on.

She turned her back to him immediately. Nearly two decades of crappy luck was enough for her to develop keen instincts when something would cause her an untold amount of trouble. Like every time her little sister said "I have a great idea," or whenever the owner of the hotel she worked for smiled and said "I know you have this covered."

Whoever that man was, he was trouble with a capital "T."

She wanted nothing to do with it—or him.

*   *   *

ALEX JEFFRIES WATCHED the little brunette scurry across the deck away from him. Everyone else waiting for their rooms seemed intent on starting the party early, despite the fact that the wind chill made the mid-March day feel like spring would never come.

He fucking hated New York.

Almost as much as he hated cruises.

Even though he knew better, he tracked the brunette's movements as she all but rushed to the harried looking cruise employee, no doubt to demand her room to get her away from the rest of the rabble. That one had high maintenance written all over her, from her pretty floral dress to her black tights and boots and the jacket that couldn't possibly hold up against this cold. She was the kind of person who dressed for visual appeal instead of function, and he'd met more than his fair share of *those* over the years.

"See something you like?"

"No." He reluctantly dragged his gaze away from her to look at Lucas. The only reason he was on this godforsaken cruise in the first place. It wasn't strictly true—Pop bought the tickets and all but strong-armed them both into coming —but if Lucas had made some excuse not to come, Alex could have gotten out of it. He *should* have gotten out of it.

Even though he knew, rationally, that his bar, Pop's, was in good hands for the next nine days, he couldn't shake the feeling that he'd arrive back in town to find it burned to the ground. That if he wasn't there every single day, putting in the time and effort, it would fall to pieces.

"You sure?" Lucas grinned. "Pop gave me clear instructions to make sure you had a good time."

"I know how to have a good time." *Too* good a time. Though if he was honest, it'd been a few years since that was true. He'd packed enough living—and mistakes—into his teens and early twenties to double the gray hairs on Pop's head, and after the old man's heart attack when Alex was twenty-two, he'd resolved not to be the cause of any more stress or worry.

That plan had backfired, though, because now Pop was convinced Alex would die grizzled and alone in the bar the old man opened. It didn't sound like such a terrible fate from where Alex stood, but telling Pop as much had resulted in these fucking cruise plans. The grandfather he'd grown up with hadn't known the meaning of vacation, but apparently Mexico was enough to loosen some of those rules, and he expected Alex to fall in line, just like always.

It was only eight days. He could survive eight days of this bullshit.

"You're right. You know how to have a good time. That's why you're scowling at everyone." Lucas sighed. "Look, man, you don't have to party on this ship if you don't want to. *I* don't plan on it. But no reason not to enjoy yourself while you're here."

Easy enough for Lucas to say. He'd always been the even-keeled friend. The one who didn't have to make a conscious effort not to fuck up every single second of every single day. The most scandalous thing about him, if it could even be called that, was that he was bi and sort of in the closet about it, but that barely counted as a "problem." When Alex fucked up, he *fucked up*, and other people paid the price.

Better to avoid all that bullshit in the first place.

Lucas sighed. "I'm not saying go full party animal. Just smile for once instead of scowling. You're going to scare someone."

Someone like the little brunette who'd all but sprinted in the opposite direction the second she laid eyes on him. He couldn't tell the color of the eyes in question, but she had the most decadent lips he'd ever seen. Pouty and plump enough to have a man thinking sinful thoughts.

If that man was interested in getting into trouble.

Alex wasn't. End of story. But as he looked at his friend, he decided maybe Lucas was right. No matter that he'd been steamrolled into his vacation, there wasn't a single damn reason not to enjoy it now that he was here. The wind chose that moment to kick up, and he shivered. "Let's get this room shit sorted and get a drink."

"There he is." Lucas clapped him on the shoulder. "Trust me. This doesn't have to be a torturous experience. You might even have fun despite yourself."

"You should take your own advice while we're here."

Lucas grinned. "Maybe I will."

An hour later, their shit in their respective cabins and drinks in their hands, they stood by the bar that shone in the low light. It was as far from *his* bar as something could be and still maintain the same label. There were no scuff marks, no stains, no *character*. Everything was streamlined and perfect and left him feeling like the only flaw in the room was his shitty attitude. He could admit, at least to himself, that this might be exactly the change of pace both Lucas and Pop claimed he needed.

They'd barely left port, but the party was already in full swing. Despite the low music, a handful of couples writhed together next to the bar, a version of foreplay he'd seen played out with college kids countless times. They were young, well on their way to being drunk, and determined to live their lives to the fullest.

He seriously hoped this ship had stocked up on condoms, or they ran the risk of a widespread STI outbreak. The thought made him turn away from the scene. Fuck, he when did he get so *old?*

And there she was.

The brunette.

She stood around a tall table with three other white women and a guy, but she was the only one he could focus on. Her dark hair shone like some kind of beacon, the sight a hook in his chest. He actually took a step toward her before he caught himself. That shit was *not* why he was here. She might be pretty in the flawless kind of way that a perverse part of him wanted to smudge, but everything from her floral dress to her pretty pale pink lipstick was a giant neon warning sign for him to stay the fuck away.

That, and the fact she all but ran from him earlier.

Alex might be a dick sometimes, but he could take a hint. He forced himself to turn back to the bar. "I think I'm going to crash early."

"Nope." Lucas shook his head. "You're going to have fun, even if I have to drag your ass around behind me."

He snorted. "Pretty sure it doesn't count as fun if you're dragging me anywhere."

"The end result is all that matters."

Hard to argue with that, and he'd been friends Lucas long enough to know better than to try. The man hadn't taken them to state in high school and leveraged a successful college football career into a full-time coaching gig because he was a pushover. When he decided he was going to do something, he did it. Which was probably why Pop had sent him with Alex on this vacation. If anyone could ensure Alex got out of his own head, it was Lucas.

Maybe they were both right. It was only eight days in the grand scheme of things. He couldn't do a damn thing now. The ship had literally sailed. Either he could bitch and moan and be the asshole that ruined Lucas's vacation, or he could try to relax a little and try to enjoy it.

Try being the operative word.

Alex managed a smile. "Does this mean you want to do shots?"

"Fuck no, man. We're too old for that shit."

His grin widened. Nothing like a little payback to brighten his day. "Shots it is!"

CHAPTER 2

"What I don't understand is how we ended up on a singles *party* cruise."

If the ship split in two and the sea swallowed Kendall, she wouldn't feel anything but grateful in that moment. She clutched her drink with both hands and tried to smile. Of them all, she would have thought that Liv would be down with a singles cruise, but her friend looked as shocked as Kendall felt. Plans were everything, and this trip was already off the rails. It made her twitch. "I finally managed to get a hold of the travel agent before we left port. She, uh, misunderstood me."

The understatement of the century. Somehow in listening to Kendall's carefully detailed list of what she wanted to accomplish on this vacation with her old friends and possible locations she wanted them to hit, the travel agent heard something totally opposite of relaxation. She *knew* she should have double- and triple-checked all the information—or, lord, booked the freaking trip herself—but then things had gone sideways at work and she hadn't had time.

She clutched her drink tighter. It was something pink and

sickly sweet, but halfway through the glass it had numbed some of her panic. "I'm so sorry, guys. I swear I thought I was booking us a nice relaxing trip. Not this." She jerked her head toward the rest of the room. Even this early, the dance floor was crowded, and the energy in the room made her fear there was another orgy-in-waiting happening.

Aubrey was the first one to smile and reach over to squeeze her shoulder. "We'll make the best of it." She looked as tired as Kendall felt, which only made Kendall feel worse. Aubrey's life hadn't gone how she planned. This *should* have been the very trip to take her mind off the fact that her dreams kept getting pushed beyond her reach by life circumstances.

Kendall looked at the rest of them. Grace and Liv and Benjamin. They'd all put their faith in her, and she'd failed them. "Maybe we can disembark on the first stop and jump onto the next *real* cruise ship that comes."

Grace shook her head. "That's not how it works."

She knew that. Of course she knew that. She just couldn't help grasping at straws. "Then maybe—"

"Maybe we make the best of it," Benjamin interrupted. He shrugged broad shoulders and gave her a small smile before casting a look around the table. "Sure, this isn't what we planned, but that doesn't mean we can't enjoy ourselves." He cleared his throat and a blush worked its way over his cheeks. "Maybe *this* is exactly what we all need."

As much as Kendall wanted to argue that a party cruise was *not* what she wanted or needed, this wasn't about her. She'd messed up. She didn't get to be the one to whine about it. So she pasted a bright smile on her face. "Benjamin's right. Let's, uh, promise to make the best of it."

She didn't miss the look Liv and Aubrey exchanged, but she couldn't decipher it. Were they just humoring her? Did they think she was overreacting? She didn't know, and because she didn't know, panic wound tighter and tighter around her. It didn't help that Grace's eyes were as wide as a deer in headlights, and she looked about two seconds from bolting from the room. Only Benjamin seemed to genuinely believe that this trip could be anything other than a disaster, and while she appreciated his support, she really, truly couldn't draw a full breath. "I'm—I need some fresh air."

"Kendall!"

She wasn't sure which of them called after her, but it didn't matter. She shoved up from the table and strode for the door, every bit of her self-control directed at making sure she didn't actually sprint from the room. Leaving that space didn't help, though. Not when she was still faced with evidence after evidence of her failure.

Kendall needed air and she needed it now.

It took her far longer than it should have to reach the deck. It was like her brain wasn't firing on all cylinders and she'd lost the instinctive navigational skills that served her so well in NYC. Or maybe they weren't skills at all, but just a habit born of her retracing the same steps over and over again.

Stuck.

She was so incredibly *stuck*.

Finally, a small eternity later, she found the right path to the top deck. Kendall stepped out into the darkness and immediately regretted the most recent questionable choice. It was *cold*. She wrapped her arms around herself and shivered. For someone who usually had a plan for everything, she'd forgotten the most important part of her wardrobe— her coat.

It didn't matter as she drew her first full breath since realizing this trip wouldn't be what she'd so desperately wanted. What she'd needed.

A break. A reset. A chance to get her head on straight and

maybe even gain a little perspective on where things had gone so wrong. Oh, her life wasn't *wrong*. She held down a good job. She had a very tiny but decent apartment. She had friends. She had her sisters, Marley and Gretchen, even if they were across the country.

But there were so many ways she didn't measure up.

She worked twice as hard as anyone else on staff and had more responsibilities than her job description listed, and yet somehow kept getting passed over for the promotion to sales manager she so desperately wanted. She did all the work, ensured nothing fell through the cracks no matter how many ill-advised hires the general manager made. And yet, everyone considered her so firmly entrenched in her assistant position that she couldn't see how she'd ever dig herself out. She felt just as trapped at work as she felt right now on this cruise she hadn't wanted.

Impossible not to compare herself to her sisters and be found lacking on both sides. Gretchen was the perfect sister, the perfect wife, the perfect everything. She was back in their little Oregon town, living her dream life because she never once diverged from the path she'd set her eyes on when she was only a teenager.

And Marley? Marley might be as unattached as a dandelion blowing in the wind, but she made no apologies for it. She drifted from place to place, never letting others' expectations box her in. She was free and bold and courageous.

Kendall? Kendall wasn't perfect, she wasn't bold, she certainly wasn't courageous. She was simply Kendall. Not *quite* good enough.

"You're going to freeze if you stay out here too long."

She jumped and spun around. Kendall blurted out a response before stopping to think. "No one asked you."

A low laugh drifted out of the darkness, followed by a man who looked vaguely familiar. It wasn't until he stopped a few feet away that she realized *why* he was familiar. The man she'd seen earlier on the deck, the one who seemed to reach across the distance and stroke her skin with his gaze.

The same way he was doing now, dragging his attention over her in a way that was just shy of being rude. He didn't linger at her breasts the way some guys would, seeming to want to take in the whole picture in equal measures.

"Stop staring at me."

He finally refocused on her face and frowned. "You should go back inside."

Consider that her skin sparked with little pricks of pain from the cold, that's exactly what she should do. What she'd planned on doing, even. But that was before this man appeared to order her around. Before she'd seen the cumulations of her "almost but not quite" life brought to a head on this stupid cruise that she'd promised her friends would be just what they needed to relax and reconnect. "I'm fine."

"Nah, I don't think you are." He considered her. "You're going to be stubborn, aren't you?"

"If by stubborn, you mean I'm going to continue with my previously intended plan, then yes, I'm going to be stubborn." She couldn't believe she'd just said that. Kendall was many things, but she wasn't the shit-starter. That was Marley. *She* was the peacemaker. The one who smoothed out all situations to make it more comfortable for other people. The one who took care of other people. She didn't bite a stranger's head off, no matter how much they aggravated her.

He laughed a little. "Thought so." He shrugged out of his leather jacket and dropped it over her shoulders before she could do more than stare.

Kendall instinctively clutched the jacket to keep it from falling off her shoulders. It wasn't the warmest piece of clothing, but it cut down the wind chill dramatically. And it smelled… She inhaled deeply. Divine. Something spicy and subtle.

"Did you just sniff my jacket?"

"No," she answered quickly. Too quickly.

Now he was flat out grinning at her like she'd done something delightful. "You did." He offered a hand. "I'm Alex."

Now was the time to leave this conversation. She wasn't on this cruise for the same reason that most everyone else seemed to be, and had absolutely no interest in any of that nonsense. And, since Kendall was the one who'd messed up, she had to put extra effort into ensuring her friends had a good time. This trip was supposed to be about *them*, about reconnecting after too much time and distance and life pushing them in different directions. The only friend from college that Kendall had regular contact with was Grace, and even then they were both so busy that they could barely manage dinner every couple of months. Maybe if she shored up those bonds, she wouldn't feel so… lost.

Alex turned and leaned against the railing, apparently content to let her stew instead of offering her name. Kendall hesitated, but finally moved to join him. "I'm Kendall."

"Kendall," he said her name like it was candy on this tongue. "What are you so afraid of?"

She jerked back. "Excuse me?"

"I've seen you exactly two times, and both times you were bolting like someone tried to set you on fire. It leaves an impression."

Because she'd all but run from him earlier, even though they'd only shared a look. She pulled his jacket more firmly around her shoulders and thanked the relative darkness of the deck that he couldn't see the embarrassment heating her cheeks. "This cruise was a mistake."

"I suspect a lot of people will be saying that by the end of it."

Because they…

She blushed harder. "I'm not dodging a mistake in human form or anything like that. I just booked this trip thinking it was a normal cruise, and I show up and…"

"Not a normal cruise." He chuckled, the sound vibrating through *her* chest as if he'd reached out and touched her. "Must have been a shock."

"You could say that." She glanced at him and her stomach dropped. "Oh god, I'm sorry. I took your coat and now you're freezing. What were you thinking?"

He turned to face her fully, and she couldn't escape the sudden awareness of how close they stood. He wasn't a huge guy, but he still dwarfed her. And that face. The moonlight seemed to caress his features lovingly, lingering on his jaw and high cheekbones. He was so attractive, it actually hurt to look at him. Kendall always thought that level of perfection best left to movie stars and people who had no business interacting with normal humans.

Alex didn't move, but he suddenly felt closer. Close enough to touch. "I wanted to talk to you a little longer."

Her whole body gave a lurch, as if every cell of her being fought to get closer to him. Kendall planted her feet out of sheer stubbornness. "I think you missed the part where I never planned on being on this cruise."

"Intentions don't mean shit. Actions do. You're here. What are you going to do about it?" As if it was that simple. Decide and act. Or maybe just skip the deciding part and act.

His words wove a siren song around her and Kendall moved without having any intention of doing it. She grasped his thin T-shirt and went up on her toes. He was still too tall to reach her destination, not without help. She made a frustrated sound.

He caught her around the waist, lifting her to him instead of descending to her. It seemed the most natural thing in the world to wrap her legs around his waist and her arms around his neck. They were so, so close, and she couldn't think too hard about what they were doing or all the ways she'd kick herself over being so impulsive tomorrow.

Instead, she kissed him.

Alex let her explore his mouth for three whole heartbeats before he took over. He turned and walked them to the wall across from the railing, pressing her there as he shifted their kiss for a better angle. His tongue slid along hers, light and teasing as if he only wanted a taste. As if he didn't have this overwhelming desperation clawing through his chest, demanding he get *closer, closer, oh my god, touch me*. The sheer force of need had Kendall breaking the kiss. "I can't."

"Okay." He started to move from the wall, started to let her down.

She tightened her grip on him. "But I really, really want to."

Alex pulled back enough to see her face. She had no idea what he saw there. His expression lay almost completely in shadow. He finally reclaimed the small space between them, settling between her thighs as if he could hold her like this all night. "You don't let your hair down much, do you?"

"My hair is down right now."

He laughed, which only made her so incredibly aware of the fact that he was hard and pressing exactly where she needed him. A little more friction, a little more kissing... God, she could orgasm just like this. Kendall pressed her lips together, not sure whether that was tempting or horrifying. Maybe a little of both.

"I have a question."

She lifted her head. "Okay."

"When's the last time you came with another person?"

It took her desire-saturated mind several long moments to decipher his words. She opened her mouth, closed it, and opened again. The truth and a lie hovered on the tip of her tongue, battling each other for the right to be voiced. Kendall finally licked her lips. "Why?"

"You're telling me that you can't do this, but you want to." His voice had gained a rasping edge, the faintest hint of an accent she was too twisted up to pinpoint. "And you're rubbing against me like you're half a second from orgasming."

To her horror, she realized he was right. While she'd been battling with herself, her body hadn't quite got the memo. She forced her hips still, forced herself to stop humping him like some kind of animal. "I'm sorry," she whispered.

"You've got nothing to apologize for."

Then why did it feel like she should? She cleared her throat. "I don't do this."

"I kind of figured that out all on my own." He wasn't quite laughing at her, but amusement colored his words. "Do you want me to let you down, Kendall?"

Yes. No.

For her entire life, her rational brain had ruled with an iron fist. First, because Kendall's grandmother had enough to deal with trying to wrangle Marley through school without getting arrested or pregnant. Because Kendall didn't want to disappoint Gretchen with her high standards and easy happiness. Then in college because she was the reliable one, the one who always took care of the people around her. And then... It just became habit.

Kendall didn't lose herself because she could never escape the little voice in her head saying she had to be the responsible one, the person to hold it all together, because her parents were gone and *someone* had to fill that void. It didn't matter that she avoided going home to Ruby Creek since her grandmother's funeral, since she couldn't stand the thought of walking those streets that housed so many ghosts, both living and dead.

"Kendall?"

"Don't stop." She wasn't sure where the surge of wildness came from, the sheer desperation to experience *something* that colored outside her lines. Just with him. Just once. Just right now. She wrapped her legs more firmly around his waist. "Please, Alex. Don't stop."

He hesitated for the space of a heartbeat as if he knew she planned to use him to escape something internal. "Fuck," he breathed.

And then his mouth was on hers again. This time, he didn't go slow and soft. He kissed her like he wanted to memorize her, like he'd never get another chance. She wasn't sure he was wrong. This moment was for tonight alone, one of the rare times when her body overrode her mind. In the light of the morning, she would regret this. She didn't care. Nothing could derail this runaway train. Not tonight. Kendall clutched his shirt, pulling him closer yet. She needed. *God*, how she needed.

Alex ran his hands from her hips to her ass and down to her thighs. He took her weight completely, spreading her a little more so he had full control. He rolled his hips, rubbing his cock against her center. Pleasure sparked through her, gathering with each long drag of him. She moaned against his lips. She couldn't help it. If he just kept doing that, she would burst apart at the seams. So close...

He didn't stop. He kept kissing her like he'd never get enough of this, and driving her inch by inch toward an orgasm that rolled over her like a tidal wave. It sucked her down, down, down, and she was vaguely away of shuddering and clinging to him and Alex pressing tightly against her again, letting her ride him and the aftershocks in turn.

Reality slammed into her the second her feet touched the deck. *Oh god, what did I just do?*

Alex saw that, too. He watched her scuttle back from him and gave a grim smile. The fact she could see her lipstick smeared across his mouth only made her feel worse. She shrugged out of his jacket and all but threw it at him. "I have to go."

"You should try to turn that big beautiful brain of yours off from time to time. You enjoy the hell out of yourself when you do."

She couldn't quite dredge up the energy to argue with him, not when her body still sang from that orgasm. *Especially* not when she ached for more. If she let this keep going, would he take her back to his cabin? Would he undress her with that confident, steady way of his and lay her down on his bed and…

She shut that thought down fast, but nowhere near fast enough. It was all too easy to transpose his pressing her against the wall to his pressing her against a bed. His hands on her body, his mouth kissing her everywhere with the same thorough way he kissed her mouth.

"You should go back to your cabin."

She blinked. "What?"

"Go back to your cabin, Kendall." He scrubbed a hand over his mouth, which only served to smear the pink color across his jaw. "You keep looking at me like that, and I'm going to kiss you again."

"Would that be such a bad thing?" she whispered. *Why* was she asking him that? He'd given her an out, the exact thing she wanted. She should be fleeing right now without looking back, not peppering him with questions that might lead to him touching her again.

"It wouldn't be a bad thing." The growl in his voice had her drifting a step closer to him. He held up a hand. "But I'm not about to contribute to a memory you use to whip yourself with. I've done enough of that already."

She wanted to argue with him, to tell him that he was wrong and she wouldn't do exactly that.

She couldn't.

Kendall forced herself back a step, and then another. "I guess this is goodbye?"

He laughed harshly. "Go. Before we both change our mind."

She made it another step. "What if that happens? We change our mind?"

"If you change your mind, Kendall, *really* change your mind, then I'm going to take you to bed." He shrugged his jacket on. "But not tonight. Go, sweetheart. Go get warm and let this shit settle."

She went.

CHAPTER 3

*A*lex spent the night alternating between a truly outstanding case of blue balls and dreams of a certain brunette all wrapped up in him. He still couldn't believe he'd sent her away. She might have been conflicted, but she wanted him. She wanted *more*. He'd wanted a whole hell of a lot more, too.

But Pop's lessons ran too deep to make that particular mistake. Even now, Alex could hear the old man's voice in his head, rasping from a couple decades' worth of whiskey and cigarettes. He'd quit both when he took over raising Alex, but the rough tone lingered.

If it's not a hell yes, it's a fuck no.

He shoved the covers off and lurched to his feet. One of the few perks of this trip was that Pop had sprung for two cabins, so Alex hadn't disturbed Lucas with his restlessness. He'd promised to try and enjoy the next week, and he couldn't do that with thoughts of Kendall dancing in his head. He could still feel her body molding to his hands, her center practically scorching him through his pants, her mouth moving desperately against his.

Alex brushed his teeth, but he swore he could still catch the lingering sweetness he tasted on her tongue last night. So he did it again. And a third time just for good measure.

A quick glance at the clock told him it was barely five in the morning. Too early to go knocking on Lucas's door, looking for a distraction. Just as well. He wouldn't make for good company until he burned off some of this energy.

Alex paused by his bag. Yeah, he'd promised to embrace the vacation mentality, but that didn't mean he'd stopped worrying about the bar. A lot of shit could go wrong in twenty-four hours. Hell, a lot could go wrong in a single hour. They didn't have much in the way of bar fights these days, not like when he was a kid and Pop catered to a slightly rougher clientele. In the last five years, Alex's renovations and careful marketing had boosted the atmosphere enough that they now brought in the upper-middle-class folk who lived around Dawson's Creek. Pops wasn't quite *trendy*, but it skirted that edge enough that he'd nearly doubled its annual earnings.

Rationally, he knew a week wasn't enough to dismantle everything he'd built. That didn't stop him from reaching for the phone and going through the process to call home.

It rang twice before a cheery female voice answered. "Thank you for calling Pop's. What can I do for you?"

"How are things going, Cherry?"

"Alex?" Instantly, the welcoming note in her voice disappeared. "What are you doing calling? You're supposed to be on vacation."

Guilt flared, but he smothered it. "I'm just checking in."

"The whole place burned down in the night."

Even though he knew she was joking, something clamped tight around his chest. There wouldn't be anything left if that happened. Nothing to rebuild. The insurance money would go to Pop, since it was his bar, and while Pop would never hang Alex out to dry, he most likely wouldn't want to rebuild.

Alex would lose it.

"Alex?" Cherry sounded worried. "Honey, I was just kidding. You're being an overprotective papa bear, and it's cute and all, but you really need to unplug and stop worrying about this place. I have it locked down."

He still couldn't quite calm his racing heart. "You know I worry."

"Just like I know that you haven't taken an actual day off since Pop moved down to Mexico. *Go*, Alex. Drink too much. Snorkel with dolphins or whatever they do on those outings. Make out with someone pretty. Just *live*. Everything will be exactly as it always is back here." She sighed. "I'm hanging up now."

"Bye, Cherry."

The line clicked and he set the phone down. Instead of making him feel better, more assured that things would roll along just fine without him, he had a whole new set of things to flip the fuck out about. If something like that happened to the bar, he'd lose everything.

Again.

He scrubbed his hands over his face. Why the hell had he agreed to come on this fucking vacation? It was a mistake. Surely Pop and Lucas would agree with him once he laid out his argument? Tomorrow, the ship would stop in Orlando and Alex would catch a flight back to Dawson's Creek. Simple as that.

But neither Pop nor Lucas would be up at this point, so he went in search of the gym. He thought better while in motion, and he knew his friend and grandfather well enough to know that he'd have to create a solid argument for them not to give him endless shit about this.

The gym was empty when he walked through the door,

which was just as well. Alex didn't have it in him to deal with another person right now. He considered his options and moved to the free weights. First legs, then he'd do arms and some core, and *then* he'd be able to think straight.

He made it through three sets of his leg routine and had just laid down on the bench for arms when the door opened. Alex bit back a sigh. With his crappy his luck was going, it just stood to figure that he wouldn't last a whole workout alone. He lifted the bar into the air and began slowly lowering it to his chest and lifting again. Matching his breathing to the steady movement was as close to meditation as he ever got, despite Cherry insisting that he could benefit from it.

To his right, a treadmill started going and quickly picked up pace. Even though he knew better—it was shitty gym etiquette—he couldn't help a glance in that direction.

He almost dropped the bar at the sight that greeted him. None other than the little brunette whose memory tormented and taunted him in turn. Kendall. She had her attention on the mirror lining the wall in front of the treadmill and she frowned like she wanted to run that other version of her into the ground. From her hesitance last night, he would have pegged her as someone who shielded themselves with layers of clothing to avoid notice. He would have been wrong. She wore bright pink shorts that hugged her ass and highlighted the strength in her legs. Her sports bra had more straps than seemed required and was a show-stopping orange. She'd pulled her long hair back into a ponytail and it swung with each steady step as she picked up her pace.

He'd thought she was gorgeous before in the sundress. Sexy in his leather jacket while she was wrapped around him like his favorite T-shirt. Alex didn't have words to describe how good she looked now.

Burning in his arms let him know that he'd held the

weight in a half-lifted position for too long. He grunted a little as he pushed it the rest of the way up and onto the rack. No way could he concentrate enough to ensure he wouldn't hurt himself with this sight greeting him.

He also couldn't sit there like a fucking creep and stare at her ass while she ran. She obviously hadn't seen him, or at least hadn't registered that it was *him*. Alex looked around the room. There was no way out that wouldn't force him to walk directly past her, and if he tried to sneak, then he'd *really* look like a creep.

Alex sat up and wiped his face with the towel he'd grabbed from the spot near the door. Only one way through this, and it was to stand up and walk out of here like he wasn't fighting his body's reaction to this woman he'd barely exchanged a handful of words with. A woman who now had sweat glistening against her skin, taking his thoughts down paths better left untrod.

He stood slowly. If he was a better guy, he wouldn't keep staring, but Alex couldn't quite tear his eyes away from her. He'd barely managed to lift them to her face when she looked up and their gazes clashed in the mirror. Kendall missed a step and slammed the big red button to stop the treadmill. She yanked out her headphones. "What are you doing here?"

The animosity in her tone stopped him short. This was awkward, sure, but they hadn't parted on bad terms last night. Right? He'd thought so, but now he wasn't so sure. Alex lifted his hands in a placating gesture. "I was working out. Same as you."

"There are laws against stalking. Lots and lots of laws."

Irritation flared, getting the best of his self-control. "Whoa there, Turbo. I was here first. It's not my fault you didn't look around before you started running, but it's not like I snuck in here with the sole purpose to surprise you. If anyone is stalking, it's *you*."

She propped her hands on her narrow hips. "A likely story."

He had no business drifting closer to her. None at all. "Are you pissed because you lost control last night? Or because I stopped us before we got what we both wanted?"

Her jaw dropped. "What? You... Why... *No*. I am not pissed at anything. I don't even know you. Last night was an aberration and I'll thank you never to speak of it again."

An aberration, huh?

Maybe she didn't do shit like make out with strangers. That was fine. He didn't, either. Not anymore. But he could see the way her attention kept drifting to his mouth, as if she couldn't help herself. And her nipples now pressed against the thin fabric of her bra. She wanted him, even if she'd probably throw herself through the glass door before she admitted as much.

A perverse part of him wanted to stay here and keep needling her until they ended up against a wall again and made a liar out of her. Instead, Alex moved to the door. "Whatever you say, sweetheart."

"That's it?" She sounded so affronted, he barely held down a grin.

He half turned as he pushed the door open. "Yeah, that's it. You don't want me to speak of it, consider the subject muted. Have a nice vacation, Kendall." Alex left the gym and headed for his cabin. Whatever this thing had been between him and Kendall, it was over. He didn't get off on convincing reluctant partners into bed, and if she wasn't reluctant, she was at least conflicted. Alex had pursued enough self-sabotage in his teens and early twenties to last a lifetime. He wasn't going to play a part in someone else's similar path.

Especially not when he had every intention of getting off this fucking ship in Orlando and catching the first flight back to Dawson's Creek.

* * *

KENDALL FINISHED her run in a fury that resulted in her fastest six miles to date. Even that wasn't enough to lift her mood. Not when she had the image of Alex tattooed into her brain. When his gaze had dropped to her breasts, to the clear indication of her arousal, she'd thought for sure he'd close the distance. That he'd take her mouth, maybe haul her over to the bench he'd just vacated and lay her down. That they'd get back to doing what they had been the night before, picking up right where they left off.

Instead, he'd left.

She unlocked her cabin door and pushed it open, but before she could walk in, the door next to hers opened. Grace stuck her head out, her dark eyes wide and panicked. "Kendall!"

Kendall froze. "Is everything okay?" If there was a problem, she could focus on fixing that instead of on the confusing feelings that plagued her whenever she thought about Alex. Which was nonstop since last night. "What can I do?"

"My clothes," Grace whispered. "I don't have vacation clothes."

"Uh... *why* don't you have vacation clothes?"

"Aubrey took my pants."

To be honest, it sounded like something Aubrey would do, at least before life kicked her in the teeth after college. A little kernel of hope blossomed in Kendall's chest. Maybe this trip wasn't such a disaster after all. She tried to dampen her delight at having something besides herself to focus on. "Then we'll get you some clothes. Give me thirty minutes to shower and get dressed and we'll go, okay?"

Grace nodded. "Okay."

As soon as she stepped into the small shower, Kendall's mind

29

betrayed her. She closed her eyes and the memory of Alex's body against hers had her going from zero to nuclear in half a second. She pressed her lips together, trying to banish him. It didn't work. Not when she swore she could still taste him, could feel his strength holding her in place as he drove her relentlessly toward orgasm. If he managed that without either of them taking off clothes, what could he accomplish if they were naked?

She skated a hand down her stomach and paused. She shouldn't. Masturbating to a fantasy was fine when she had time on her hands and didn't have a friend waiting for her. Doing it to an actual person she'd just had a conversation with this morning? Wicked. Wrong. So naughty, she could barely stand it.

Kendall let her hand continue its southern journey until she stroked her clit. With her eyes closed and the water cascading over her sensitive skin, she could almost imagine it was Alex's hands on her instead of her own. More. She needed more. She pressed a finger inside, but it wasn't enough. She'd known it wouldn't be enough even before she did it.

She opened her eyes. Somehow, the fact that she was on a time limit, that she shouldn't be doing this for half a dozen well-documented reasons, only made it hotter. She turned off the shower, gave herself the barest wipe down, and walked naked to her suitcase. She'd packed her vibrator on a whim, telling herself it was just in case of emergencies.

Well, if this didn't count as an emergency, she didn't know what did.

Kendall laid on top of her comforter and spread her legs. Instantly, her memory of Alex morphed into something more. She pictured him spreading her thighs wider and pressed the vibrator to her clit, pictured him looking at her like he had last night, all shadows and temptation and desire.

And then he lowered his head and kissed her between her thighs.

She came with a muffled cry, riding out the vibrations that somehow weren't as good as she was sure Alex's mouth would be. Kendall gasped and rolled to the side, all but flinging her vibrator away. What was she *doing*? She didn't do this. Any of this. It had to be the pheromones on the ship or something they were pumping into the air ducts to ensure everyone acted as foolishly as possible.

She dressed quickly, throwing on a pair of high-waisted shorts and a button-down top that she tied around her waist, revealing a tiny sliver of skin. As she dragged a comb through her hair, she tried to tell herself that she wasn't hoping to run into Alex.

After pulling on her sandals, she headed to Grace's door to knock. Her friend barely let Kendall's knuckles make contact before she hauled the door open and stepped into the hall. "Let's go."

"Sure." Kendall fell into step next to her, hoping like hell that she wasn't blushing as hard as the heat beneath her skin suggested. No way could Grace know what she'd been doing a few short minutes ago, but she felt like it was written all over her. A scarlet letter of sorts, one she couldn't help wanting to repeat over and over again.

Alex's words from last night echoed through her, deep and dark with a hint of growl. *If you change your mind, Kendall, really change your mind, then I'm going to take you to bed.*

"Kendall?"

Oh god. She was so busy focusing on her illicit attraction to a near-stranger that she wasn't focusing on the friend in need right next to her. She shoved her hair back and tried for a smile. "I'm sorry. I guess my mind is still all preoccupied with how I'm going to make this all up to you and the others."

Grace gave her a strange look. "We can start with finding me some clothes."

She glanced at the clothes her friend currently wore. A sleeveless blouse and a pencil skirt. They weren't bad, as such things went. Grace always had an impeccable sense of style, even when they were in college. She just looked...buttoned up...but then Grace *always* looked buttoned up. Despite her angst about her pants theft, she still looked perfectly put together today, if a little restrained.

Kendall cleared her throat. "I know Aubrey took your pants, and I agree that was kind of a dick move." Even if she silently agreed that *someone* had to take intervention, she'd never been one to trample boundaries like that. Some days she wished she was that brave. "But since we're all determined to make the best of this trip despite all the issues... Why don't you buy shorts instead of pants?"

Grace wouldn't quite meet her gaze. "I'll think about it."

She wanted to press for confirmation, but Kendall forced the words back. It wasn't right for her to hyper focus on fixing Grace just to distract herself from her issues. Or, rather, from one issue in particular.

As they went through the shops to find clothing that Grace would be content in, Kendall found herself thinking about Alex again and again. He was so unlike the other guys she'd met over the years when she went through fits of loneliness dark enough to try the various dating apps. Some of them had been losers, for sure, but there were nice ones thrown into the mix. A few even turned into third and fourth dates before they drifted apart. She hadn't cared enough to fight to stay close, and they obviously felt the same.

But Alex?

She really couldn't imagine that man using a dating app,

or sitting through an awkward first meeting, or sending a dick pic. He was too cool, too confident, too at home in his skin. He had to draw people to him like flies to honey.

Kendall made a face. Guess that made her a fly. It wasn't the most flattering comparison, but how else to explain her fascination with the man? She dragged her fingers through her hair and tried to focus as she and Grace headed back toward their cabins. She was being a bad friend by thinking of herself while Grace was in crisis mode. At least Grace seemed calmer now that they were done shopping, more settled on the idea of not replacing her pants.

She had barely closed the door to her cabin when her gaze landed on the bed. On what she'd done there while thinking about *him*. Kendall's body gave a pulse and she shivered. She had no business wanting this man, especially considering how she'd freaked out on him in the gym. *He* wouldn't want *her* anymore.

She took a deep breath. Yes, that's exactly right. Better to focus on that than on her confusing impulses around Alex. She just needed to deal with this trip and the rest would figure itself out.

Feeling settled for the first time since yesterday, she changed into her swimsuit and pulled on her floral cover-up. A quick stop by the others' cabins let them know where to find her. Then she went up to the pool deck and staked out a few chairs. Not the most difficult thing to do. Even at midmorning, the place was mostly deserted. If she was a betting woman, she'd bet that most of the people took advantage of the *party* part of the party cruise last night and were sleeping it off.

Just as well.

Kendall lathered herself up with sunscreen and pulled her floppy hat out of her tote bag. Holding it in her hands made her chest pang. Her grandmother had one just like it when

Kendall was growing up. Whenever the stress of life—and raising her three granddaughters—got to her, she'd throw on her silly floppy hat and go spend time in the garden. When Kendall was old enough to understand that her grandmother didn't want conversation during those times, she was allowed to work beside her. When she pictured peace, she pictured the warmth of those days, the coarse dirt against her fingertips, and the joy of seeing plants she'd cultivated growing enough to bear fruit and vegetables.

Her little kitchen garden in New York wasn't the same thing at all.

God, she missed her grandmother. Had been missing her every day in the years since she'd passed. She just *knew* if Gram were still alive, she'd have words of wisdom that would help Kendall make sense of where her life had gotten so messed up. Maybe she'd even be able to pinpoint the exact moment Kendall zigged when she should have zagged. Maybe she'd even have advice on how to get back on the right path.

Except Kendall didn't know what the right path was. Not anymore.

She could call Gretchen. Her older sister was full of sage wisdom, even if she was only a few years older than Kendall. She didn't exactly resent her sister for living a charmed life— marrying her high school sweetheart, being totally happy in the small town they grew up in, beloved by most people she came across. It just wasn't Kendall's path. She'd mostly made her peace with that over the years, but it meant Gretchen's advice came with a big dose of salt. They were different people who wanted different things, and sometimes her big sister forgot that.

She plopped the hat on her head and sank onto the lounge chair. Figuring out her life would have to wait. Right now, she had some intense relaxing to do. The others would hopefully show up later, but right now she could let her guard down a little and sink into a good book. Kendall adjusted her sunglasses and pulled her e-reader from the tote bag. She'd gone on a book-buying binge before leaving for the trip, so she had approximately twenty romance novels waiting and nothing but time for reading in her future. This might not be the perfect vacation she'd planned, but she was *determined* for the rest of it to go off without a hitch.

Surely that wasn't too much to ask? Yes, there were two people who appeared to be having sex on a lounge chair on the other side of the deck, but she didn't have to look at them. Or listen.

Oh god, this was a nightmare.

CHAPTER 4

*A*lex wandered the ship for hours. It really was a floating city, and maybe if he was at a different point in his life, he'd be more impressed. As it was, he couldn't quite distract himself from worrying about the bar back home. Not even knowing how disappointed Pop would be was enough to snap him out of it.

Pop's intentions were good. They always had been. But he and Alex were just different people. Pop might be content to hand his pride and joy off to another person, even if it was Alex, but Alex couldn't stand the thought of everything that would inevitably go wrong without him present. Cherry was good at her job—he wouldn't have hired her if she wasn't—but she wasn't *Alex*.

He stepped out onto the deck and took a long breath. They'd moved south far enough to leave behind the cold of the upper East Coast, and the sun seemed so much bigger here. Warmer. Closer to what it was like at home. He considered calling the bar again, but Cherry had stopped answering after the third call today, when she told him she had it handled and to kindly fuck right off. He wished it was that easy.

Alex moved from one deck to another, a meandering path that he'd have to end at some point. He should check in with Lucas, though his friend hadn't responded when he'd knocked on his door earlier. Maybe Lucas actually *was* getting in on some of the party cruise action. Good for him. Alex actually kind of hoped he was, because it would make his leaving in Orlando easier if Lucas had a reason to stay on the ship.

He stopped short, his attention landing on the woman hidden beneath an atrocious hat. Even without seeing her long dark hair, he recognized Kendall. He had the sudden thought that he'd recognize her anywhere, but that was bullshit. It had to be. He barely knew this woman.

Even as he told himself to keep walking, to not linger where he wasn't wanted, Alex drank in the sight of her in a bright red bikini. Her skin was pale enough that either she didn't get out much, or she religiously applied sunscreen. He suspected it was a combo. The empty chairs on either side of her held a bag and a towel, as if she wanted to reserve them for some of her friends. Judging from the way her skin glistened, she'd been out here for quite some time.

Something twisted in his gut at the thought of this woman waiting for people who never showed. She already felt like a person who stood apart. She didn't need more isolation.

Alex veered toward her before he could think of all the reasons it was a bad idea. She looked up as he sank onto the chair next to her and groaned. "Oh god, I thought this couldn't get any more embarrassing, and then you show up to prove me wrong. Again. Is that a super power of yours? Because it's a really crappy one to have."

He blinked. Her words weren't *quite* slurring, but she'd

just spilled them as if they were a river inside her, instead of biting them out like she normally seemed to do in his presence. "You doing okay?" Alex asked carefully.

"That's a stupid question." She flopped back onto her lounge chair, her large hat temporarily concealing her entire face.

He took the opportunity to lean down and sniff her drink. Something fruity that most definitely had alcohol in it. A *lot* of alcohol.

"What are you doing?"

Alex lifted his head. From this angle, he was looking up at her and... Damn, Kendall really was something. Her cheeks were rosy, whether from drink or the heat, and she pursed her lips at him in a disapproving frown he suddenly wanted to kiss off her face. "How long have you been drinking?" The juice in there wouldn't be enough to combat the alcohol and heat when it came to hydration, and the sugar just fucked stuff up more.

"I'm on a *party* cruise, Alex." She waved a wobbling hand at the rest of the deck. It was still early enough that most people out there were either hungover and recovering or just getting started, so the deck was still half deserted. "I've watched no fewer than four couples have sex in the last two hours. Honestly, you'd think they'd be worried about sunburn or people knowing *exactly* what they're doing under that towel, but *nope*. They just go at it. It's a *party cruise.*"

"Yeah, you mentioned that."

She hiccupped. "I'm just embracing the party, since I don't have another freaking choice."

Wow, she was totally wasted. "Kendall, how long have you been out here?"

"I don't know. A while."

He'd seen her in the gym hours ago. Surely she hadn't come straight here? Shit. Alex looked around, but no one materialized who seemed to know her. No, her friends would be no help right now. "We need to get you some water and out of the sun." Some food wouldn't hurt, either, depending on how her stomach handled the water.

"I'm fine."

"Tell me that again when you stand up." He pushed to his feet and held out a hand. "Come on. If you keep going, you're going to be in a world of hurt for the rest of the day and most of the night. You need a nap."

"Is that a euphemism?" She stumbled over the word, rolling it over her tongue until she found its shape. "Because I am not sure I want to have sex with you right now?"

Alex cursed the bolt of lust that shot straight through him. This woman needed help, not him drooling over her like a horny college kid. He wiggled his fingers. "Come on, Kendall. Or I'm going to have to track down one of your friends. Don't think it'll be easy since I don't know their names or anything about them. It'll probably require a ship-wide announcement for the friends of Kendall—What's your last name, sweetheart?"

"Barnes." She slapped her hands over her mouth. "Wait, no. I didn't mean to say that."

He injected a little authority into his tone. "Would the travel companions of Kendall Barnes please come to collect her?"

Her jaw dropped. "You wouldn't dare."

That told him everything he needed to know. Kendall would do anything to avoid causing a scene. He might be a bastard to use that against her, but it was for her own good right now. "I one hundred percent *would* dare."

"Oh, you…" She fumbled around, shoving her things into the tote bag that looked big enough to cart several medium sized animals around in. "You *jerk*."

She really was too precious. Alex took her bag and helped

her to her feet. He watched her closely, which paid off when she took one step and tilted wildly. "Hold up." He caught her around the waist and barely kept them from toppling over two lounge chairs as they made their way off the deck.

"You could, you know."

He glanced down at her. "Could what?"

"Seduce me." Kendall blinked at him, but he couldn't tell if she was trying to be seductive or attempting not to pass out.

He swallowed past his suddenly dry throat. "I'll keep that in mind." Not right now, while she was drunk as a skunk, but maybe she didn't see him as quite the mistake she'd acted like last night.

"It was supposed to be a nice cruise." She leaned heavily on him, her head lolling against his shoulder. "Nice. Relaxing. Really nice."

"A nice cruise. Got it." He had to adjust his grip around her waist, and it was impossible not to notice how good she felt against him. His hand slid against her skin and he had to scramble to keep her on her feet. "Sweetheart, we're taking a right turn."

She immediately veered left, and he had to tug her in the opposite direction. "The other right."

"Right, right, left, right, left." She giggled. "Left my wife with twenty-one kids and thought it was *right*, right, left, right, left."

This woman was just full of surprises. "Is that a marching cadence?"

"Yep. Grams had a gentleman friend who was a veteran when I was ten and he taught it to us." She giggled. "Grams was far more amused than she should have been, but then Grams was really fond of dirty limericks, so I suppose she wasn't one to throw stones at what was child appropriate."

He picked apart that sentence as he guided them through

the doors and toward the elevators. "Your Grams sounds like quite the character."

"She was." She released a long breath. "I miss her."

"I'm sorry."

"Don't be." She frowned. "Is that pizza?" Suddenly, Kendall wasn't leaning on him quite so hard. "I could really go for about six slices right now."

Alex fought down a laugh. "Let's start with one and see how it goes." He guided her to a table and eased her into a chair. "Sit here. I'll get you pizza and some water." He eyed her. The icy blast of air conditioning already had goosebumps rising in a wave across her skin. "You have one of those swimsuit things?"

"A swimsuit thing?" She blinked big green eyes at him. "I'm wearing one right now." Kendall looked around. "Oh god, is there a dress code? I'll take it off." She fumbled for the straps.

"No!" He caught her hands. Holy shit, his heart was beating entirely too hard for this shit. Alex was no stranger to dealing with drunk people, but he usually didn't worry overmuch if they made asses of themselves. His job wasn't to preserve their dignity; it was to ensure they weren't harmed while they were in the bar, and to get them home safely if at all possible. That was it.

But he knew without a shadow of a doubt that Kendall would die of mortification if she did something like take off her top while drunk. In the few encounters they'd had to date, she came across as wound so tightly, she was one wrong move away from bursting her seams. He shouldn't care. Hell, Alex's entire morning had been wrapped up in worrying about the bar. He had a lot on his plate, and didn't need to add this woman, too.

And yet...

"Cover-up." That's what it was called. "Where's your cover-up?"

"Oh!" She brightened, giving him a sunny smile. "Right!" Kendall wiggled her hands out of his and pulled a floral piece of cloth from her giant bag. She stood, weaving a little, and wrapped it around her body. Between one blink and the next, it became a dress. Somehow. With another bright smile, she pointed at the counter. "Food!"

"Your wish is my command." It took him a few short minutes to place her order and return with the food and water. He dropped into the chair across from her and slid the water over. "First, water. Drink slow."

"I'm not an amateur, Alex." She bent down for the straw and missed. "Silly straw." Kendall cupped her drink in two hands and brought it to her lips with the carefulness of a person just realizing how shit-faced they were. "I'm drunk."

"Yes, sweetheart, you really, really are."

"I never get drunk. Ever."

He leaned forward and propped his elbows on the table. They'd got her out of the sun and she was taking small sips of water without any issue, so he could afford to relax a little. In theory. "Why not?"

"It's messy."

No arguing that. "Sometimes it's good to let loose."

Kendall's face fell. It might have been amusing if it didn't break his heart the tiniest bit. "I don't know how to do that. I'm too uptight. A planner. The responsible one that everyone depends on." She rattled off the descriptors with the familiarity of someone who heard them enough times for the traits to be printed on her soul. As if they made her a little sad.

It wasn't his business. *This woman* wasn't his business. He had every intention of leaving the ship tomorrow when they docked in Orlando. If Alex was smart, he'd hand her off to one of the staff and go on his way without looking back.

But would that staff member be invested in her safety? They'd drop her in her room and that would be that. Or, more horrifying to even think of, they might… take liberties. No. Fuck that. Alex would ensure she sobered up safely and then he'd go to his room and double check that he hadn't forgotten to repack everything. At least if he knew Kendall was delivered safely to her bed, he could stop worrying about her.

Probably.

But that was later, after she'd eaten something and got a little more water into her. He slid the slice of pizza across the table. "That's bullshit."

"What's bullshit?"

"You're on a party cruise and drunk before noon. I would hardly call that responsible and uptight."

She gave him a slow smile that lit up her face. A man could go blind from the way she beamed at him, the same way he could go blind by staring into the sun. Kendall picked up the pizza. "You really think so?"

"I know so. I run a bar. I know exciting when I see it." Even if that was exactly the thing he tried to avoid in Pop's. Excitement usually translated to drama and bullshit and, when his luck was particularly bad, into bar fights. Alex worked hard to draw in a different clientele, to boost the reputation of Pop's and bring it into this new hipster era that seemed like it wasn't going anywhere anytime soon. It meant fewer bar fights and more drinks thrown in assholes' faces on first dates, but that was a trade-off Alex was more than happy to make.

She ate for a few minutes, and he thought she'd moved on, but when Kendall finally set her half-eaten slice down and sat back, she blinked at him. "You own a bar?"

"No." The word burned like a physical thing on his tongue, but he ignored the sensation just like he ignored it every other time he answered this question. "My grandfather owns it. He's just enjoying his retirement in Mexico and so I run it for him now."

She tilted her head to the side, her long fall of dark brown hair sliding over her shoulder. "It's hard to let go of them, huh?"

The empathy in those big green eyes hit him like a shot to the chest. He absently rubbed the spot as if he could soothe away the sudden ache there. "What are you talking about?"

"Grams died while I was in college." Her full lower lip quivered before she steadied herself. "It's not the same thing, but I miss her every day."

Alex sat back. What was he supposed to say to that? Yeah, he missed Pops, but the missing was all tangled up in abandonment and responsibility and other shit he wasn't about to dig into. He didn't begrudge the old man his retirement. Not exactly. "I miss him, too." That, at least, was the truth. The rest of it could stay internal. This woman needed to be taken care of right now, not to have him pour his emotional bullshit all over her.

He nodded at her plate. "You good?"

"If I eat any more, I'm going to burst."

Somehow, he doubted that, but from the way her blinks kept getting longer and longer, if he didn't get her out of that chair immediately, she'd pass out right here and now. "I'll walk you back to your cabin."

"That's either sweet or super creepy." She let him tug her to her feet and slid under his arm as if she had every right to be there. He wasn't sure she was wrong, at least in this moment. It felt nice to have her tucked against him, even if the only reason she was there was because she was too fucking drunk to walk on her own.

Alex led her away from the table and looked around. "Which way?"

She rattled off her room number, completely oblivious that it was rule number one in personal safety—don't just give that fucking information out. God, she was like a baby foal right now, all fumbling movements and blind trust. It made him want to wrap her up and tuck her away until the bristling woman with the prickly walls came back. *She* wouldn't blithely give out personal information to a near-stranger.

By the time they got to Kendall's room, he was half carrying her. He helped her unlock the door, but when he went to release her, she nearly fell on her face. Okay, this wasn't going to work. He cast a look around, but the only person in the hall was some dude six doors doing who gave him a thumbs up like carting some semi-unconscious woman into a room was a good thing. Alex glared until the guy turned on his heel and fled. He waited another minute, but no one else showed up, let alone one of the people who'd been at her table having drinks the night before.

There was no help for it. He sighed. "Guess I'm on babysitting duty for a little while longer."

CHAPTER 5

Kendall was pretty sure something had died in her mouth while she slept. Her tongue felt fuzzy, too. Maybe she had contracted one of those horrible diseases that they tried so hard to keep from spreading through a cruise ship? The thought had her opening her eyes and shooting up to a sitting position.

Or attempting to.

Her head pounded and why was the light so freaking *bright?* She threw her hands over her eyes. "Oh god, *why?*"

"Best guess? Vodka."

The male voice next to her had her reacting before her brain caught up with the fact she recognized it. Kendall flew backward and would have tumbled off the edge of the mattress if a hand didn't close on her wrist and haul her back to relative safety.

Though she hardly called being on her bed with I'll-give-you-an-orgasm-with-all-your-clothes-on Alex… She didn't even know his last name. God, she really had embraced this party cruise thing a little too hard and they were only twenty-four hours in.

She looked down at herself. Her bikini was still covering the essentials. A close look at him found him in a pair of shorts and a truly absurd Hawaiian print button-down. "What's going on with your shirt?"

He looked at it and grimaced. "Pops's style has changed more than a bit since he retired."

Some of the fog on her brain shifted, and she remembered him mentioning his grandfather. "I thought he retired to Mexico, not Hawaii."

"Don't try to think of it from a logical point of view. I gave up years ago."

"Okay," she said slowly. "Let's try another one. Why are you in my cabin?" They hadn't had sex. She *knew* they hadn't had sex. Kendall flinched as another memory emerged; her telling him that he could seduce her. "Actually, hold that thought." She all but sprinted into the little bathroom and shut the door.

One look in the mirror painted her as the mess she'd suspected she was. Her hair was tangled, her lips were chapped, and she had the worst breath in living memory. Kendall wasted no time brushing her teeth while she quickly cataloged her condition. No sunburn, thank goodness for the 100 SPF she'd coated herself with before laying out. Her headache had already faded a little, but the two Tylenol she popped the second she finished brushing her teeth would fix the rest of it.

The temptation to hide in the bathroom until Alex took a hint and left was strong—really strong—but she couldn't repay his unexpected kindness by being a coward. No matter how much she wanted to. Kendall took a deep breath, allowed herself a full five seconds to regret the fact that she'd chosen a bikini instead of something that covered a bit more skin, and opened the door.

To find Alex standing a few inches away.

She bit down a shriek. "What are you *doing?*"

"You might not remember this, but you weren't walking too well a few hours ago. I was hoping I wouldn't have to bust down the door and save you. Again." He searched her face, his blue eyes intense.

She must have had some residual alcohol swimming around in her system. It was the only excuse for her saying, "You are too gorgeous to be real."

Alex grinned. "Saying stuff like that is a good way to convince me that you hit your head."

Now was the time to walk him to the door and then spend an hour berating herself for her carelessness in getting drunk like that. So drunk she needed a near-stranger to take care of her. At least none of her friends had been there to witness it, but somehow that didn't make it better. This whole trip was supposed to be to reconnect with them, and they'd managed a single dinner and drinks before they scattered to the winds.

Just like after college.

It wasn't their fault, not really. The excursions and stuff didn't start until tomorrow and they all had things they wanted to do on the ship. Begrudging them for doing those things instead of spending time with her was selfish. When the ground felt a little steadier under her feet, she'd stop feeling so bad about the whole thing.

Probably.

"What's put that look on your face, sweetheart?" Alex frowned down at her, his perfect dark brows drawn together in a way she shouldn't find charming, but she most definitely did. "You've got nothing to feel bad about. You're on a party cruise, so getting a little tipsy and having the sun go to your head is to be expected. It was a little harmless fun, and you're safe."

He'd gone out of his way to ensure she was safe. Even

now, when she was far too sober for her current thoughts, Alex wasn't looking to press his advantage. He wanted to reassure her so she didn't have a boatload of regrets for her shitty choices.

This guy really was something else. Something *rare*. Something she'd be an idiot to pass up, even if it was only a once in a lifetime kind of thing.

Kendall licked her lips, suddenly nervous. "Alex?"

"Yeah?" He still frowned at her like he was afraid she'd burst into tears or something.

Was she really going to do this? She opened her mouth to thank him and tell him to please leave, but those weren't the words that rose in her throat. No, her id had fully taken over, and instead she said, "Take me to bed."

He froze. She was pretty sure he stopped breathing entirely. "What?"

"Take—Take me to bed?" She couldn't close the distance between them, wasn't brave enough to use more than her words to put this offer on the table. Kendall might be feeling adrift and reckless, but even now, there were lines she couldn't quite make herself cross. She took a shuddering breath. "I… I want you."

Still, he looked at her as if he wasn't sure she hadn't downed a bottle of tequila in the few minutes she was in the bathroom. "Kendall—"

"Shut up and kiss me!"

They stared at each other in shock. Had she *really* just yelled at him like that? Anxiety rose in a wave, quickly followed by regret. She knew better than to put herself out like this. Alex had shown himself to be a legitimately not horrible person and here she was, demanding that he kiss her like some kind of monster. She opened her mouth to apologize.

Alex didn't give her a chance to.

He closed the distance between them and slid his fingers through her hair, tilting her face up to his. She got a glimpse of something like agony in his blue eyes and then his mouth was on hers and she couldn't focus on anything but the slow slide of his tongue unraveling her completely. How could he do more with a kiss than some of her past boyfriends had done with their entire bodies? She didn't understand it.

That was almost enough to have her pulling back despite being the one to instigate this. She cautiously ran her hands up his chest. He wasn't one of those men who possessed carved muscles and an unreal body. No, Alex was all too real. Her knees went a little weak and he caught her around her waist with one arm. The shock of skin on skin had her pulling her mouth from his. "I don't know what I'm doing."

Alex gave a wry smile. "You don't do this kind of thing. I remember."

God, she'd said that, hadn't she? Kendall gripped his shirt and tried to think past the wild pounding of her heart. "That sounds really slut shame-y and I didn't mean it like that. I don't ... let go. I don't know how to."

Instantly, his expression softened. "We don't have to do anything, sweetheart."

If she didn't do something drastic, and do it soon, he'd walk out of her room because of misguided honor. Kendall tightened her grip on his shirt. "I didn't mean it like that, either. I *want* to do stuff. I'm just going to be awkward and probably talk too much and ruin the moment."

"I see." He considered her. This guy might give off the bad boy vibe, but she'd never had a man listen the way he did, even in the few interactions they'd had. What other man would take care of her sloppy drunk self and stay until she woke up to ensure she was okay? None of the ones she'd dated.

If that wasn't depressing, Kendall didn't know what was.

Alex stroked her hip almost idly, still watching her closely. "Sex is still off the table."

"*What?*"

"Yeah." He nodded, almost as if talking to himself. "You've got to learn to walk before you start running. You'll still regret it if we have sex now."

She drew herself up. It would have worked a lot better if she wasn't standing in her bare feet and only about as tall as his shoulder. Kendall didn't care. She stoked the flicker of irritation, using it to shield something like hurt in her chest. "Alex, you're really cool."

"Thanks."

"But don't think for a second that you get to decide what I am and am not ready for. I'm an adult. If I regret something, I'll own that, but you don't get to make that call."

"Fair." He grinned. "Okay, how about a counterproposal?"

She narrowed her eyes, mock-glaring at him even as she tried not to smile. "I'll consider making a counter-counter-proposal once I hear your proposed terms."

He stroked her hip again, letting his fingers play against her skin just above the ties of her swimsuit. "Let me make you feel good again. Just that."

Her body zinged in response. She nodded a little too fast. "Deal."

Alex's chuckle vibrated through her. "Sweetheart, you're shit at bargaining."

"Am I?" She let him back her toward the bed. "Because I'm pretty sure I have an outstanding orgasm in my near future, so who's the real winner?"

"Me," he said seriously. And then he lifted her up and moved them both onto the bed. Kendall had exactly two seconds of *Oh god, I shouldn't be doing this* and then Alex's weight settled down on top of her and she nearly moaned. Forget sex, she was starved for human contact. If she wasn't careful, she could fall asleep just like this, with this man anchoring her to earth. Alex leveraged himself up a little and took in her expression. "What are you thinking?"

"That you're the sexiest gravity blanket in existence."

He laughed. A full, deep laugh that rolled through her like a bell tolling. "That would be some side hustle."

"You could make a fortune." She reached up, feeling tentative all of a sudden, and touched the buttons on the front of his Hawaiian shirt. "Can I?"

"Go for it."

She undid them quickly despite her shaking hands. It took a little maneuvering to get the shirt off him completely, but then Alex settled fully against her, so much of his skin against so much of hers. This time, she couldn't hold back a moan. Mortification heated her cheeks and spread across her chest. No way he missed the way she'd gone beet red, but Alex just laid a series of gentle kisses along her jaw and down her neck. "You don't take care of yourself."

"I…" Her breath hitched when he nibbled on the spot where her neck met her shoulder. "Sure I do."

"Nope." He traced down the line of her bikini top with his mouth but bypassed her breasts to kiss down her stomach. "Maybe you take care of your body, but you hold yourself apart. It hurts you."

His words struck far too close to home. She propped herself up on her elbows. "I signed up for orgasms, not for therapy."

"You might consider it."

"A therapist?" She blinked. "Are you licensed?"

"No, but I'm the next best thing." Alex settled between her thighs and looked at her with those intense blue eyes. "I'm a bartender."

"I… see." Except she didn't see. Not at all. What was his game? If he just wanted to have sex with her, he had a strange way of going about it. He certainly couldn't want *more*. The man was on a single's party cruise for god's sake. No one in their right mind would book this trip if they wanted something serious.

What was she even thinking?

She'd just gone from zero to sixty in the space of thirty seconds. What she really wanted was for Alex to do what he promised and make her feel good. That was it. Anything more was out of the question. Her life just didn't have room for another person. She'd tried that—more than once—and it never worked out, usually because her work required so much of her that there was nothing left over for her partner. So she'd stopped trying. Really, it was better that way. She was happier alone.

Mostly.

Kendall cleared her throat. "If you want to have this conversation, I'd rather not have it when you're right *there*." His shoulders kept her legs spread and his face was so, so close to the apex of her thighs.

For a second, she thought he'd decide he'd rather talk than continue the scorching path with his mouth. She held her breath, waiting to see what he'd do. Alex gave her one last long look and then dipped down to press an open-mouthed kiss to the sensitive skin just above her bikini bottoms. He moved to her thighs, kissing and nipping as he nudged them wider.

There wasn't enough air in the room. Kendall watched him touch her, kiss her, and couldn't look away. Pleasure washed over her, priming her so intensely, she thought she might be able to come from this alone. The thought brought a wave of embarrassment, but she pushed it away. "Alex, please."

He paused, his mouth against skin. "Yeah?"

He was going to make her say it, wasn't he? No gray areas

with this man. He was more than willing to give her what she wanted, but he required enthusiastic consent to get them there. She might appreciate that later, when she wasn't about to go out of her skin with wanting him. Kendall cleared her throat, and it still took two tries to get the words out. "I want your mouth on me."

Still, he waited.

Kendall pressed her lips together and took a slow breath. She could do this. She *could*. She reached down and untied both sides of her swimsuit. "Make me come. Please."

He surged up and caught her mouth. The unexpectedness of it made her squeak, but she relaxed into the feel of him almost immediately. He kissed her hard, and she couldn't shake the feeling that he was claiming her in some way she'd never quite comprehend. It was too much and not enough and she didn't understand any of this.

Maybe that was the point, though.

Alex, damn him, seemed to know exactly what she was thinking. He reached between them and snagged her swimsuit, and then he pulled it off her, baring her from the waist down. She didn't have a moment to feel strange about that because he was already moving down her body to resume his position. Except this time nothing served as a barrier.

She held her breath, praying he wouldn't make her wait, and someone upstairs must have been listening because this time Alex didn't tease her. He gave her pussy the same thorough kiss he'd just given her mouth, exploring her with his tongue. Savoring her.

He growled and the sound made her writhe. As if he couldn't contain his desire any more than she could. As if maybe he wasn't as in control as he seemed. He urged her legs wider and spread her so he could fuck her slowly with this tongue. "You taste good, sweetheart. A man could lose himself in you if he's not careful."

She blinked, barely able to comprehend his words. He almost sounded like he thought she was some temptress, but that couldn't possibly be right. She was Kendall freaking Barnes, and she rarely broke the rules, let alone indulged herself with something as decadent as being on the receiving end of stellar oral sex from a man who was barely more than a stranger.

"You're thinking too hard." He lifted his head. "We still good?"

"Yes, we're good." She might die if he didn't keep going, but he showed no signs of resuming. Kendall licked her lips. "I don't know how to stop thinking so hard," she whispered.

Alex gave her a wicked grin. "I have a few ideas." He went back to her clit, working her with the flat of his tongue. And then he pushed two fingers into her.

Kendall's thoughts shorted out. Her whole world went fuzzy and then narrowed down to the way he filled her even as he kept that motion against her clit that had tension coiling through her. "Don't stop."

This time, Alex had no verbal response. He didn't pick up his pace, either, didn't rush her to the finish line. He just kept up those languid strokes as he rotated his wrist and made a motion inside her that had her whole body going liquid. "Oh god." She forgot to worry about what he might think and dug her fingers into his hair, holding him in place. "Don't stop. Please don't stop."

He didn't stop. He drew her inexorably to the edge and then pushed her over, sending her hurtling into an orgasm that wracked her body. Her grip on his hair spasmed and she ground her pussy against his mouth, mindlessly seeking to prolong the pleasure.

As she drifted down, Alex slid his fingers out of her and gentled his kisses. She expected him to... Well, she wasn't sure what she expected. This man never seemed to do what she anticipated.

She certainly didn't anticipate him climbing up to lay on the bed next to her and then tucking her against his body. A little maneuvering and he flipped the comforter over them, cocooning her in warmth. She tried to tense up, but her body didn't get the memo. Instead, she sprawled across him as he trailed his fingers up and down her spine.

Kendall started to reach down, to move to return the favor, but Alex caught her wrist. "It's okay, sweetheart. This was about you."

That pulled her out of her euphoria a tiny bit. She lifted her head. "Are you going for saintly status or something?"

"No." His chuckle was a little strained. "Nothing like that. I said I'd make you feel good. I wasn't part of the bargain."

"And you say *I'm* a crappy bargainer." No reason to feel hurt that he didn't want her to make him come. None at all. But it didn't stop the feeling from crawling through her. Was this just a pity orgasm? *Another* pity orgasm?

God, she really was that pathetic, wasn't she?

CHAPTER 6

*A*lex wasn't sure when things went so sideways, but as he lay there with Kendall in his arms and a set of blue balls for the record books, he couldn't bring himself to regret it. Every instinct he had about this woman was proving correct. Wound too tightly. In desperate need of letting go even more than he supposedly was. But once she did let go?

He shifted, even knowing damn well it wouldn't do anything to relieve the aching of his cock. She'd had every intention of getting him off, but a strange part of him didn't want this to be transactional. Tit for tat. He hadn't been thinking about his pleasure when he towed her to the bed, and he sure as fuck hadn't thought about getting his rocks off when he had his mouth all over her pussy, or when she came so hard that she about took his fingers off.

"You should probably go." Kendall's breath hitched, and Alex froze. Holy fuck, was she going to cry? Nowhere in how he thought this would play out did *crying* come into the picture.

Shit.

Shit.

Had he missed a sign? Had he just fucked up beyond belief?

Alex forced his body not to tense and kept his tone even. "What's wrong, sweetheart?"

"Nothing." Kendall cleared her throat, and when she spoke again, she seemed to have herself better under control. "It's nothing."

His heart actually stopped. He was sure of it. "Doesn't sound like nothing from where I'm sitting."

"Then maybe you should change your perspective."

There she was. He liked it when she showed her claws. Even knowing her as briefly as he had, Alex suspected she didn't get snarly with people as a general rule. He couldn't stop himself from running his fingers through her hair. "You having regrets?"

"No. It's nothing like that." But the wobble was back in her voice.

Damn it, she *was* having regrets. Alex stared at the ceiling, trying to weigh out the best path forward. Did he take off and give her time to find her footing again, or would that cause more damage than staying? He didn't know. Hooking up wasn't something he did much anymore, and never with someone like Kendall. When Alex needed his itch scratched, he found a partner who wanted the same thing. Someone who would be intent on their mutual pleasure, instead of worrying about the morning after.

Kendall wasn't like that. As she kept telling him, she didn't *do* this. Didn't let go. Didn't fuck around. Didn't do any of it.

"You want to talk about it?"

She huffed and sat up. "If I did, I'd talk to my therapist, not to some random guy I met fewer than twenty-four hours ago."

That stung, but he ignored it. "Fair enough." He made a show of looking around. "I don't see your therapist, so… next best thing?" Kendall still wouldn't look at him, and actual fear curdled his stomach. "Kendall, sweetheart, talk to me. Did I… Did I hurt you?" He hadn't thought so. She'd seemed like she'd enjoyed every second of it, and she'd definitely come, but he should have known better than to take her up on her offer when she was so clearly hurting from something. Even if Alex wasn't the initial cause, he'd contributed to that pain.

"What?" She finally twisted to face him, a frown drawing her brows together. "Hurt me?"

Her honest confusion didn't make him feel any better. "You were fine. Now you're not. Only one thing has changed." He waved a hand between them. "Hard not to draw conclusions from that."

Some of her consternation cleared, and she sighed. "Alex, why don't you want me?"

It took him a full five seconds to process her words, but they still didn't make any sense. "Of course I want you." When she still didn't look convinced, he gave a choked laugh. "I about came in my pants just from you orgasming on my face."

"Then why…" She made a vague wave at his cock, still standing at attention.

Comprehension dawned. It wasn't the sex that fucked her up. She'd seen his turning down her offer as a rejection. "Kendall." He waited for her to meet his gaze to continue. "I want you. I want you so fucking bad, it was everything I could do not to take you up on *everything* you offered and sink into that tight little pussy of yours until I can feel you come around my cock."

She blinked. "I still don't understand."

God, she was killing him. "You keep telling me you don't

do this. You've obviously got some shit going on, and I don't want to be something you regret." Adding to the burdens she carried wasn't on his agenda, and yet that's exactly what he'd accidentally done. He didn't know how to fix this, or if he should even try. With his track record, he was just as likely to make it worse as he was to make it better.

"I don't get you." She pulled the blanket more firmly around her, covering her body nearly completely. "Like are you even real? Because at this point, I have my doubts."

That surprised a laugh out of him. "I'm real, sweetheart."

"If you say so." She frowned. "I think I might be the one being an asshole right now, and I'm not sure how that happened."

"Hey." He waited for her to look at him. "Come here."

Kendall slowly, almost reluctantly, settled back against him. He managed to keep the tension from his body, to not wrap her up and hug her until she felt better about this whole thing again. He didn't want to be something—someone—she regretted. A silly thought, maybe. He had every intention of leaving this ship behind and not looking back once they docked in Orlando in the morning.

The thought didn't bring him the relief it had earlier today. He gave into the urge to wrap his arms around Kendall and cuddle her close. Another thing he didn't normally do. Easier for everyone when sex was clearly just sex and not edging into anything messy. Sometimes he cuddled his partners, sometimes not, but most of them preferred the latter. He'd never felt the lack before, but now he couldn't imagine walking away from Kendall before he had a chance to smooth this out. The scent of her floral shampoo wrapped around him, and he mentally cursed himself for pulling her closer when all his cock wanted to do was sink into her.

Not today. Not like this.

Then when?

There would be no other opportunity. Not when he had every intention of cutting his vacation short.

She finally sighed and all the tension bled from her body. "I just wanted to reconnect with my friends. We were so close in college, and since then everyone is so busy all the time. I'm just as bad as everyone else, so I'm one hundred percent not throwing stones, but I miss them. I thought this was such a brilliant idea to spend more time together, but I managed to mess that up and booked us the wrong cruise."

She'd mentioned something like that earlier, but he was too busy trying to keep her from walking into a wall to pay too much attention. "No way do they hold this against you."

"I don't think it's that, exactly." She snuggled closer almost absently. "It's just not what I thought it was going to be. Nothing about this is. I should have realized that a cruise would offer them all sorts of things they want to do beyond lying by the pool, but I didn't really think about it. Even though we didn't have finalized plans today, it still feels bad that I was alone."

He couldn't help giving her a squeeze. Alex had never wanted to be good at comforting and the softer set of people skills, but he did right in that moment. Surely a squeeze was helpful? He just didn't know. "I'm sorry."

"It's fine." The wobble still in her voice said otherwise. Kendall gave herself a shake and propped up on her elbow. "How did you end up on this cruise? It doesn't seem like your kind of thing."

"It's not." He let himself drink in the sight of her, enjoying the way the twinkle came back into her green eyes. "My grandfather thought it would be a good present to force me to take a vacation, but *this* was his idea of a good vacation."

Her eyes went wide. "Your *grandfather* is on this cruise?"

"What? No." He laughed and it felt…good. "No, Pop said

this kind of shit would be bad for his heart." He gave their intertwined bodies a significant look. Alex's heart wasn't doing too great at the moment, either. His cock still hadn't calmed down, but he gave that up for a lost cause. A little agony never hurt anyone.

She smiled. "That's a fair point. I admire his moxie. My younger sister might think something like this was a brilliant idea, but I'm pretty sure my older sister would die on the spot if she was on the ship."

Moxie. That was one way to describe Pop.

"He thinks I work too much." Alex didn't mean to say it. But then, he didn't mean to do a lot when it came to this woman. Right now, he should be making his excuses and establishing that this was the end of the road for them. He should be telling her that he wouldn't be around for the rest of the cruise.

He should be doing a lot of things.

"Do you?"

"Probably." He shrugged as much as he could in his current position. "Who doesn't these days?"

"That's the freaking truth." Kendall seemed to argue with herself and finally said, "Thanks."

"For what?"

"For all of it. Taking care of me this morning. The two orgasms. All of it." She lifted her face and he had to bite back a smile as how hard she was blushing. Kendall pressed her lips together and finally said, "I would really, really like to return the favor."

Alex's mind shorted out as what little blood remained in his body rushed to his dick. He took a slow breath, trying to battle his desire. Trying and failing. "You don't have to do that."

"I know. Like I said, I *want* to." She didn't give him a chance to argue. Kendall shifted to straddle him, and his honorable intentions died a noble death. She gave him a little smile as she went for the front of his shorts.

They both froze as someone knocked on her door.

A woman's voice came through, soft and worried. "Kendall, are you in there?"

Kendall paled and leaped off Alex like his body had caught fire. "Oh my god, you have to hide." She looked around frantically. *"Right now."*

* * *

KENDALL COULDN'T BELIEVE this was happening. She'd managed to get through high school without ever sneaking a boy into her bedroom, let alone being caught while doing it. Now, at thirty, she was reduced to shoving Alex into the bathroom and shutting the door behind him.

Which was right around the time she realized she was mostly naked.

She spun around, searching for her bikini bottoms. Meanwhile, Grace knocked again. "I know you're in there. I can hear you rustling around. Open the door, Kendall." Then, softer. "I'm sorry I didn't make it to the deck in time to catch you. Something came up."

"Just a second!" Kendall dug through her suitcase and pulled out a sundress. She ripped off her bikini top and yanked the dress over her head. Going without a bra, let alone without panties, wasn't the least bit comfortable, but it was better than the alternative. She cast a quick glance at the closed bathroom door, but Alex didn't seem to be in any hurry to betray his presence. It'd have to be good enough.

She ran her fingers through her hair and pasted a smile on her face as she opened the door. "Hey, Grace."

Grace nearly bowled her over as she pushed into the room. "I'm sorry."

"It's fine."

"No, it's not. I said I'd be there and then I wasn't, and no one has seen you since this morning and—"

Kendall grabbed Grace's shoulders and waited for her friend to look at her. "It's fine. I drank a little too much and came back here for a nap. It's a cruise. It stands to reason that people got distracted or chose to do other things besides lie out by the pool." Her words sounded reasonable, but that didn't stop the twist in her gut at the thought of her friends wanting to do other things besides hang out with her. Whoever said that people eventually outgrew the feeling of being a hanger-on to their friends was a liar. Hard not to believe that when the evidence pointed to exactly that.

Stop it.

Easier said than done. She tried for a smile. "It's really okay."

"No, it's not." Grace seemed to finally take in her appearance, and her dark brows rose. "You look—"

"I was taking a nap," Kendall said firmly.

"A nap," Grace repeated. If anything, her brows rose higher. "There's beard burn on your chest."

She released her friend and slapped her hands to her chest. "No, there's not."

"Yes, there really is." Grace turned and examined the cabin. Kendall could practically see her cataloging the details with that impressive brain of hers. She toed the untied bikini bottoms on the floor. "Did he leave right before I got here, or is he hiding in the bathroom?"

"*Grace*. What the hell?" She crossed her arms over her chest, which only served to remind her what a freaking liar she was. "I do not have a guy in my room."

"Uh huh." Grace took a step back. "Then I guess you won't mind if I…" She darted to the bathroom door and opened it before Kendall could do more than screech. Alex stood there shirtless, a shit-eating grin on his face. Grace's eyes went wide. "Holy crap, you have a man in your bathroom."

"No, I don't. This is all a figment of your imagination." Could a person die of humiliation? Because Kendall had to be approaching dangerous levels at this point of the trip. She could *not* believe this was happening.

If anything, Alex's grin widened. He held out a hand. "I'm Alex, and apparently I'm imaginary."

"Grace." She shook his hand and gave him a once-over. "Apparently I'm interrupting."

"No. No, you are most definitely not interrupting." Kendall reached around Grace and grabbed Alex's arm. "Thanks for the help back to my cabin. I'll just..." His laugh made her face flame hotter. "Bye!" She opened the exterior door and all but shoved him out, and then slammed it behind her. Kendall turned around and pressed herself against it and glared at her friend. "I can't believe you just did that."

"*Me?* I can't believe you tried to hide a man in your bathroom!"

She couldn't believe it, either. Now that Alex was gone, she had the strange thought that it really was all a dream, after all. Surely she hadn't had a near-stranger bring her to orgasm with his mouth and hands just a little while ago? Surely she hadn't fully intended on doing the same to him? She shivered. God, she really needed to put some panties on, but she couldn't figure out how to do it without admitting to Grace that she wasn't wearing them to begin with.

Kendall cleared her throat. "Where were you this morning?"

Just like that, Grace's amused expression fled. "Nowhere," she answered too quickly.

"Nowhere," she repeated. "That sounds like a story."

"It's not. At all." Grace was...blushing.

Kendall forgot all about her own mortification and focused on her friend's. "Sounds like there's a story there."

For a second, it seemed like Grace wouldn't spill, but she let out a long exhale. "Yes, there's a story there, and if we leave *right now* I'll tell you about it on the way to dinner. Come on, we're going to be late if we don't hurry."

She had no choice but to follow her friend out the door. Alex was nowhere to be seen, and she told herself the feeling in the pit of her stomach was relief and not disappointment. She hadn't seen him at dinner last night, so he probably had a different time slot than they did. Or maybe she just hadn't been paying attention? Kendall wasn't sure, but she couldn't help looking for him as they walked to their table.

Right as they reached the table where the rest of her friends sat, her gaze landed on a familiar pair of blue eyes. Alex had found time to change and he sat next to a cute white guy who had *athlete* written all over him, but all his attention seemed focused on her. She blushed and then cursed herself for blushing.

She and Grace took the two saved seats, but Kendall couldn't focus on the conversation going on around her because she kept sneaking glances at Alex. Somehow, being in the same room as him made her a thousand times more aware that she had nothing on underneath her dress. She picked at her food and tried to pay attention, but it wasn't until Liv said her name that she lifted her head. "What?"

Liv gave a pained smile. "Sorry we weren't there this morning."

"It's fine." She realized how short she sounded when Liz and Aubrey exchanged a look. Kendall forced her tone to brighten. It wasn't their fault that nothing on this trip had gone according to plan. "Really, it's totally okay. What's the point of a cruise if you can't do all the things without having to worry too hard about schedules? With five people, it's hard to organize that kind of stuff, so really there's nothing to apologize for. We didn't even technically have plans."

Grace gave her a significant look, but no way was she outing herself to the rest of her friends. Bad enough that one person knew what a cliché Kendall had become. She beamed at the rest of them. "Speaking of plans—are you doing the Orlando day trip tomorrow?"

The conversation turned to that, and she sagged back in her seat. Best if she made her peace that this trip wouldn't be anything like she'd planned. No one seemed to be having a terrible time, and that was all that mattered. Wasn't it?

She cast a look in Alex's direction even as she told herself not to. He pushed out of his seat, gave her a significant look, and headed out the door. What did *that* look mean? Kendall pressed her thighs together. She didn't know, but she wanted to find out.

CHAPTER 7

*A*lex had every intention of going back to his room and crashing. It was the smartest way to spend the time between now and when he got off this fucking boat. Except... That wasn't what he did at all. He headed back to the bar where he'd seen Kendall last night. It wasn't particularly crowded, not yet, so he found a spot in the corner where he could watch the rest of the room. Just one drink and then he'd go back to the cabin. Sure. Right. A devil's bargain if he'd ever made one.

Fifteen minutes later, Kendall walked through the door. Just like he'd somehow known she would. She looked around the room before her gaze settled on him, and then she squared her shoulders and headed in his direction. It gave him plenty of time to drink in the sight of her. She wore the same thing she'd had on when she kicked him out of her room earlier, another floral sundress thing that kissed the tops of her knees with each step and hugged her breasts in a way that told him she wasn't wearing a bra. She'd managed to tame her hair, at least a little bit, but she still looked like she'd been thoroughly fucked and enjoyed every minute of it.

Not for the first time, he wondered why the hell he hadn't taken that last step. What was stopping him? He wanted her. She obviously wanted him or she wouldn't keep seeking him out. They were two consenting adults. The math all added up to her riding his cock until they exhausted themselves.

And yet...

She stopped in front of him and took his drink out of his hand. Kendall downed the tequila and winced. "Oh god."

"That's my drink," he said mildly.

"I know." She gave him a strained smile. "I was hoping it'd give me some courage."

Courage? He went still. Somehow, Alex knew beyond a shadow of a doubt that every moment of the last forty-eight-ish hours had been leading them to this point. They stood on the edge of a cliff and one wrong move would send them toppling over.

Or one right move.

He watched her closely. "Did it?"

"Yes." She stepped forward, right between his thighs, and leaned up to whisper in his ear. "I'm not wearing any panties."

His hands settled on her hips as if they were meant to be there. Maybe they were. Alex had only had half the drink but he still felt a buzzing in his veins as if he'd just downed an entire bottle. He dragged his palms down over her ass, the thin fabric confirming her statement. Kendall was standing between his thighs in a room full of people with no panties on. And she wanted him to do something about it.

He rotated on the bar stool, taking her with him, until her back was to the bar and his thighs hid her hips from the rest of the room. Not that anyone was paying attention. The low lights had people pursuing their own pleasures, whether it was conversation and drinks or flirting and kissing. It seemed like every time he turned around on this ship, he caught sight of people in various stages of fucking. He and Kendall were just two among many.

He kept one hand on her hip and dropped the other between them to trace a path up her thigh. Alex stopped just beneath the hem of her dress. "You want me to do something about it."

"Yes." She carefully placed her hands on his chest and shifted closer. "I want you to do something about it."

He shouldn't. Now was the time to put the brakes on, to tell her that she couldn't expect anything from him because in a few hours, he'd no longer be on this ship. "Kendall—"

"All my life, I've been *good*. I've bent over backwards and twisted myself into knots to ensure I didn't make waves. I don't step out of line, Alex. Not once. I've never done anything purely because I want to." She fisted her hands in his stupid Hawaiian shirt. "I want this. I want *you*. Just for a little while." She looked up at him with those big green eyes. "*Please* stop being noble for ten seconds and *touch me*."

The carefully created leash holding him snapped. "I'm not noble." He delved beneath her dress and cupped her pussy roughly. "There is nothing about me that's noble, Kendall."

"Prove it."

He pushed a single finger into her and then two. "I should bend you over this bar in front of everyone. Push up that skirt and take what you're offering me."

Kendall tried to spread her legs to allow him deeper, but he held her caged. Tormenting them both. She licked her lips. "Or we can find a storage room and I can... suck your cock."

His whole body went white hot and his vision grayed out for half a second. The image of her on her knees, watching him as she wrapped those sinful lips around his cock nearly had Alex coming in his shorts. He withdrew his fingers and circled her clit. "Not yet. First..." After a quick battle with himself, he shifted her, maneuvering her leg closest to the wall up over his thigh. Her dress still covered her, but the position left her open for him. He resumed fucking her with his fingers and began circling her clit with this thumb. "First I'm going to make you come right here. Try not to scream."

Against all reason, she laughed. "Do it."

For someone who didn't step outside the lines, she sure was determined to throw herself into things head first. He loved it. He slowed his strokes, wanting to make this last. Kendall always looked beautiful, but in this moment, she was wild and free and unencumbered. She wanted to feel good, and he wanted to be the one to do it.

Alex leaned down and kissed her. He couldn't help it. Being this close and *not* tasting her seemed like a Herculean task. She met him eagerly, all lingering tequila and desire. That brought him up short. He lifted his head. "How much have you had to drink since you woke up."

"*Alex.*" She whimpered and rolled her hips, trying to get him to resume his movements. "I had your tequila. That's it." When he still didn't move, she huffed out a sigh. "I promise, okay? Please just don't stop."

Maybe he should question her more, but she was a grown ass woman and she wasn't showing any signs of being intoxicated. Not like she had this morning. He had to trust her. Fuck, he had to trust himself when it came to this. He shifted to nip her ear and started finger fucking her again. "You dirty girl. You knew you were going to seek me out, didn't you?"

"Maybe," she breathed.

"No maybe about it." He twisted his wrist, seeking the spot that would send her hurtling over the edge. "Did you spend all dinner debating with yourself about whether you should find me?" Her body shook and he wrapped an arm around her waist, keeping her steady. "Have you been aching and empty, needing my cock?"

She buried her face in his neck and clung to him, but that

wasn't good enough. He wanted to hear her say it. He *needed* to hear her say it. "That wasn't a rhetorical question, Kendall."

"Oh god." She whimpered again, and then her mouth was on his neck, trailing kisses up to his jaw. "Yes, okay? It's only been a couple hours and I can't stop thinking about the way you touched me. I feel like I'm drugged. I can't get enough. I want more, Alex. I want you to make me come right here, and then I want you to take me somewhere and..." Her breath hitched. "I want you to fuck me. I want it so bad, I can't think of anything else."

Fuck.

He closed his eyes, but that only made what remained of his control waver. If he wasn't careful, he'd haul her up to straddle him and then he'd be inside her right here and—No. She hadn't signed on for that and he wouldn't even be considering it if he wasn't so crazed right now. They had to get out of here, and they had to do it now. He stopped teasing her and picked up his pace. "I won't leave you wanting, Kendall. You'll get everything you need and more."

She kissed him as she came, her body riding his fingers in a way he wished he could lean back to watch. He didn't know Kendall. Not really. It seemed beyond comprehension that this woman embracing her orgasm with such enthusiasm was the same one who claimed to never make waves, to never *live*.

Something surged in his chest, but he fought it down. It didn't matter that he liked her. She wasn't for keeping. Fuck, *Alex* wasn't for keeping. The people in his life had proven that time and time again. He loved. They left. End of story. The only true consistent was the bar, and only because its foundations kept it in place in a way people lacked. Even Pop walked, though the old man more than earned his freedom from Alex after all those rough years.

No, he would give Kendall what she asked for. What she needed. He'd make sure it was good for her, that she didn't have any regrets when this was all over.

Can I manage that in a single night?

He pushed the thought away. No use thinking about leaving tomorrow when he had her in his arms right now. Alex shifted her leg down and smoothed her dress. A quick glance around showed no one paying them any attention. He pressed a soft kiss to her lips. "Let's go back to my cabin."

"But... the storage closet."

He gave a strained laugh. "Kendall, the things I want to do to you need a bed and a few hours at least." He nudged her back so he could stand. His cockstand wasn't going away anytime soon, but he adjusted himself so he could walk without too much agony. "Let's go." He took her hand and towed her after him.

He needed to be inside her, and he needed it now.

* * *

KENDALL HAD ABSOLUTELY no reason to be frustrated. She'd just come in the most decadent, wicked way possible—from Alex's hand in the middle of an increasingly crowded bar. He had every intention of having sex with her tonight. Sex that took *hours*. She should be floating on cloud nine.

Except...

They reached the elevators and she grabbed Alex's wrist before he could punch in his floor. Instead, Kendall pushed the button to take them to the deck. He watched her in that careful way he had sometimes, where he looked like he was trying to read her thoughts. "Did you change your mind?"

"No." Part of her wished she could blame her boldness on alcohol like she had this morning, but Kendall had no such safety net right now. The half shot of tequila had been all placebo effect. She stepped into him, her chest to his. "We don't have to find a storage closet. I'm not even sure they have them on this ship. I mean, I'm sure they do, but—"

"Kendall."

"Right. Sorry." She dropped her gaze to his ridiculous shirt, but he used a single finger beneath her chin to lift her face until she met his eyes. No getting out of this, then. Her skin went warm in a way strange combination of desire and embarrassment. It seemed to be her default on this trip. She took a slow breath. "This might sound silly, but I want to be wild."

His lips quirked. "I'd say what you just did was plenty wild."

She could almost believe that he wanted to protect her, but that seemed to be reaching. Then again, Alex had shown himself to be just as noble as she'd accused him earlier. Why would that stop now? "What you described earlier." Her skin flared even hotter, but she made herself continue. How could she expect him to take her seriously if she could barely choke out what she wanted? "I don't think I'm an exhibitionist enough to want that, exactly." Another fortifying breath. "But I want the illusion of that."

The elevator door dinged behind them. Alex walked her backward out of it, his hands on her keeping her steady and balanced. "You want to pretend we're fucking in front of people."

"Yes," she whispered.

He kept them moving, though his gaze barely left her face. She couldn't tell what he was thinking from his expression, couldn't figure out if he thought she was ridiculous or if it was hot or... She didn't even know. Maybe this was a mistake.

This is most definitely a mistake.

She shoved the tiny voice away. This whole cruise was a

mistake. Why not embrace it at this point? She was so tired of fighting losing battles. Some days, it felt like her entire life was just a string of battles she was destined to lose. At work. At home. With her friends. Tomorrow, she'd find the morose thoughts dramatic, but right now, when she didn't know what Alex was thinking, they felt entirely too real.

He finally stopped them. She looked around to find that they'd reached a far part of the deck. There were lounge chairs here, like in other parts, but they were wreathed in shadows. Kendall's heartbeat kicked up another notch. "Please say something."

"I'll make you a deal." He sank his fingers into her hair and tilted her head back. Eliminating her ability to hide from him. "I'll give you whatever you want, Kendall. While we're on this trip, it's yours. All you have to do is ask for it."

Her breath caught in her lungs. The sheer power he offered her... Had anyone ever done that for her before? She couldn't concentrate while being this close to him, but she didn't think so. She licked her lips. "Okay."

"What do you want?"

Her brain fumbled through the words, and her mouth wasn't much better. "You. Me. Sex. Here."

Alex gave a small smile, though the intensity in his eyes might create an inferno right there where they stood. "Tell me how."

Oh wow, he was really going to make her say it, wasn't he? She let loose a breathless laugh. She could do this. Really, she could. "The lounge chair. I want to..." *Come on, Kendall.* "I want to ride you."

His grip spasmed on her hair, the only outward sign that he was just as into the idea as she was. "I don't have a condom, sweetheart."

"I do." She awkwardly reached between them to dig into the front of her dress. Shoving a condom down her top had felt absolutely ridiculous when she'd done it in the bathroom before coming up to the bar, but she was so glad she had now. Kendall waved the foil packet in front of his face. "Apparently the cruise took out stock in condoms because they're everywhere."

"Thank fuck." He took it from her and slid it into his pocket. "Come here." Alex sank onto the lounge chair and *holy crap, they were doing this.* He tugged on her hand, and she carefully straddled him. It felt strange and a little awkward, but then Alex hooked an arm around her waist and hauled them both back so he was against the half-reclining back of the lounge chair and she was flush against his chest.

Oh. She could work with this.

Kendall went for the front of his pants, but Alex gave a muffled curse and caught her wrists. "Slow, sweetheart. You grab my cock right now and I'm going to lose it."

Something warm flowed through her, more intoxicating than any alcohol she'd had on this trip. It felt like... power? "You want me that much."

He gave a strained laugh. "You have no idea."

Her awkwardness dissipated in the face of how easily Alex admitted how affected he was. By his desire for her. By *her.* It was so far from the polite sex she'd had that she almost laughed. If she'd told one of her previous partners that she wanted to have semi-public sex, they would have driven her to have her head checked by a doctor instead of actually considering it. Alex barely even questioned her, and only to confirm that it was exactly what she wanted.

"I'm beginning to get the idea." She settled against him, her breath catching in her throat at the feeling of his cock pressed against her. They'd been a similar position before. She knew she could get herself off like this. It wasn't enough, though. As amazing as the orgasms he'd dealt her to date were, she wanted more. She wanted it *all.*

She wanted Alex crazed enough to give it to her without holding back.

Kendall looked over her shoulder. They weren't quite alone on deck, but the other pair on the opposite side of the pool, almost out of sight, was occupied with each other. From the faint moans she could tell no one was watching. No one saw when she slipped the straps of her dress off her shoulders and let it fall to her waist, baring her breasts to Alex.

"*Fuck*," he breathed.

"That's the idea."

Another of those strained laughs she was learning to love. "You sure you don't live on the edge? Because you're killing me, sweetheart. I'm trying to do right by you."

He might claim he didn't have a noble streak, but every time he said something like this, he proved himself a liar. Kendall took his hands and guided them to her breasts. "You *are* doing right by me. All I have to do is ask, remember? I'm asking, Alex. Let me ride you." Every time she spoke her desires, it became easier. Hotter. She leaned forward, pressing into his rough palms. "I need your cock inside me, filling me up."

"Dirty girl." He shifted his grip and surged up, capturing her nipple with his mouth. He sucked hard and laid his teeth against her, making her grind down hard on him. It was so good and yet nowhere near enough.

"Alex, *please*."

"Next time," he muttered. "Next time we get a bed." He pulled the condom out and ripped the foil open.

"Yes, yes, yes. Next time. Bed. I promise." She undid his pants and withdrew his cock and, god, it was even better than she'd dreamed. Perfect. He was simply perfect. "I don't want to wait anymore."

"Yeah, I got that." He rolled the condom onto his cock and

fisted it. "You want to ride my cock, sweetheart? It's here, ready for you."

She shifted up, paused, and dragged her dress up enough so she could watch him notch himself at her entrance. Could watch as she sank down inch by torturous inch, her body fighting to accommodate his size. *More, more, more.*

"Whoa, Kendall, slow down." He caught her hips. "I don't want to hurt you."

"I don't want to slow down." She grabbed his shoulders and slammed herself down the rest of the way, sheathing him to the hilt. Kendall shook as the fullness nearly overwhelmed her. It had been... a very long time since she had sex. And last time hadn't been anything like this. Even knowing she should wait, should let herself get used to this, she rocked her hips. "More."

"Jesus." He gave a choked laugh. "You're going to kill me."

"I might kill me, too." She couldn't get enough air in her lungs. "Alex..."

Somehow, he understood. He relaxed back by inches and slid his hands up her thighs, bunching her dress around her hips and allowing her to free her hands. "You're in charge, sweetheart. Take what you need from me."

She braced her hands on his chest and began to move slowly, simply enjoying this moment. This control. Alex was one big line of tension beneath her, and she had the sudden thought that he was fighting himself in order to give her this. She straightened a bit and arched her back, giving him a show. "How long can you hold out?"

"As long as you need," he gritted out.

If she wasn't careful, she might fall in love with this man. It didn't seem to matter that she didn't know him. That they hadn't talked about anything in depth. That he was little more than a stranger. He showed her the truth of himself in a thousand different ways every time he touched her. Every time he put his needs on hold so she could come first, could feel safe, could have a sliver of control.

Kendall ground down hard on his cock, unable to stop her moan. "You feel so good. Better than I imagined."

He grunted in response, his fingers digging into her hips. Not guiding her. Just hanging on for dear life. It made the whole experience exponentially hotter, which should have been impossible.

Teasing him made her a special kind of evil, but she couldn't help it. She wanted that control to snap the same way it had in the bar. She wanted him to let go the same way he allowed her to let go. "Do you feel me, Alex?"

"I feel you, sweetheart." He spoke through clenched teeth.

Not enough. She cupped her breasts, plucking at her nipples as his gaze narrowed on her. Pleasure spiked through her, but it wasn't enough. Not like this. Not with him holding back. She bit her bottom lip. "I want…"

"Tell me."

An idea occurred to her. "I want it like you described in the bar. Take me from behind."

He cursed and, for a moment, she thought he might do exactly that. But Alex gave a sharp shake of his head. "Fuck that. I want to see your face when you come again." He shifted his grip to stroke his thumb over her clit. "You look so fucking beautiful right now. Free. Wicked. Like a goddamn fantasy come to life."

Had anyone ever called her a fantasy?

She didn't even have to think hard to know the answer. No. They hadn't. She wasn't wicked. She wasn't a fantasy. And free? The thought might make her laugh if she wasn't so close to coming. She picked up her pace, determined to take them both over the edge. "You make me feel like that."

Something like regret flickered over his face, gone too fast for her to be sure. "It's all you, sweetheart."

She didn't believe him, but she suddenly didn't have the breath to argue. Kendall's body took over, her need to come shorting out her ability to do anything but mindlessly ride him, pressing hard against his thumb and slamming down to take him deep inside her.

Her orgasm hit her between one breath and the next, bowing her back and making her cry out, careless of who might hear. Alex surged up beneath her, gathering her into his arms and burying his face in her neck as he fucked her from below, slamming into her again and again until he came with a curse. He slumped back on the lounge chair, taking her with him.

Kendall lay there, listening to the pounding of his heart against her ear, and couldn't stop a stupid grin from spreading across her lips. She'd done this. She'd been wild and free and everything Alex seemed to think she was. Even if this only lasted for the rest of the cruise, surely that was enough? A little slice of the life she might have had if she wasn't Kendall Barnes, the middle child, the responsible one, the woman who didn't make waves.

When she could draw a full breath again, she lifted her head. "Alex?"

"Yeah?"

"You know how you said that I could have anything I wanted as long as I asked?"

Again, that flicker on his face. "Yes."

She could do this. She could ask for what she wanted. She didn't have to feel weird about this. Kendall swallowed hard. "I would really like for you to take me back to your cabin."

She was pretty sure he stopped breathing. "For sex or…?"

Oh god, had she made a mistake. She started to sit up, to retreat, but his hold tightened on her. "I'm looking for clarification, sweetheart. That's all."

Right. Okay. No reason to freak out and think he was

rejecting her. She closed her eyes and reached for courage. "For sex and for sleeping. If that's okay?"

Silence for a beat. Two. Three. Just when she thought that surely she'd misread the situation and he was, in fact, rejecting her, Alex said, "That's more than okay."

CHAPTER 8

*A*lex woke up with Kendall in his arms. He turned his head enough to see the alarm on the nightstand and silently cursed. The ship had already docked in Orlando and the excursions started shortly. He snorted. Excursions. Most cruises went to exotic places—and this one would, too—but Orlando hardly seemed that.

Or maybe he was just bitter because he hadn't planned on being on this cruise to begin with.

Kendall made a sound in her sleep and shifted closer. She rubbed her nose against his chest like she wanted to burrow, and he shouldn't find it so fucking endearing, but he just wanted to gather her up and keep her safe. And, yeah, he wanted to bury his cock in her again and again until they were too exhausted to keep going. Despite her offer last night, she'd passed out the second she was horizontal in his bed, and he couldn't bring himself to be annoyed about it. Not when he got to wake up like this.

What the fuck was he thinking?

He was supposed to leave today. That was to be the grand plan. Take off during the excursion and catch the first flight back to Dawson's Creek. To reassure himself that the one constant in his life was still up and running and hadn't been ruined in his absence.

He couldn't quite dredge up the energy to get out of bed, though. Not with this woman here, not when last night she became this fledgling wild thing that he wanted to experience again. Kendall had obviously spent her entire life buttoned up. This cruise—with him—she finally let her hair down. She *trusted* him enough to do it. If he left, would he hurt her? Would it drive her back into her shell again?

It wasn't his responsibility, but guilt still wrapped around his throat and squeezed. He didn't want to be the reason she never let out her wild side again.

Kendall tensed, a sure sign that she was no longer asleep. She slowly lifted her head, her green eyes wide. "Hi," she whispered.

"Hey," he whispered back. This, as much as everything else, felt intimate. Like they were the only two people left in the world. He had no business liking it, but damn it, he did. "You sleep okay?"

"Uh... Yes?" She inched back from him, and he released her. "Did I... Did I drool on you?"

He couldn't help grinning. "Only a little."

"Oh god." She flopped onto her back and threw an arm over her eyes. "Every time I think I can't be more mortified in front of you, I go and prove myself wrong. At least I didn't snore?"

Really, it was too easy. "Just tiny little snores. They were cute."

She lifted her arm and shot him a look. "You're messing with me."

"Yeah."

"Thank goodness." She let her arm flop back down. "Do I want to know what time it is?"

Time. The one thing he both needed to and desperately didn't want to focus on. Alex glanced at the clock again. If she left now, he could get packed and make it to the excursion departure with plenty of time. He considered the woman in his bed, considered what waited for him back home...

And made a decision.

"You mind if I make a call real quick?"

"Go for it. I'm going to..." She waved her other hand in the vague direction of the door.

It should be exactly what he wanted, but he shook his head. "Stay. Unless you have plans already." He hesitated. "Or don't want to."

Kendall sat up, seeming unaware of the way the sheet slid half down her breasts, teasing him with the very edges of her pink nipples. "I can't tell if you're being polite or if you really want me to stay."

Fuck, she was killing him.

Alex climbed out of bed and reached for the phone. "I wouldn't ask you to stay if I didn't want you here."

"Okay." She considered him. "I'm going to borrow your toothpaste, though."

"By all means." He waited for her to go into the bathroom and close the door to dial the bar. Despite the early hour, it only rang twice before Cherry answered. Alex barely let her get the greeting out. "I need an update. A real one."

Cherry huffed out a breath. "Good morning, Alex. It's so nice to hear from you *again* despite the fact you're supposed to be on vacation."

"Cherry." He sank enough warning into his tone to have her growling at him.

"Yes, things are fine. Just like they were fine last night. Just like they'll be fine for the remainder of your vacation. For god's sake, Alex, it's summer. People are too busy suffering from heat exhaustion to cause trouble, and even if they could work up the energy, I have a full staff that *you* trained who are capable of handling it." She paused and her tone went a little soft. "You need this, okay? So stop being a pain in my ass and go actually *enjoy* yourself."

She made it sound like it was the easiest thing in the world. "It's not that simple."

"It's exactly that simple." He could almost picture her stern frown and the way her perfectly penciled eyebrows had to be drawing together right about now. "Alex, go find yourself someone to have fun with for a few days. You never know what could happen in the time you aren't chained to this business. *Live* a little."

He didn't tell her that he'd done more than enough living in his teens and early twenties. That his bullshit antics had put Pop in the hospital with a fucking heart attack. Cherry wouldn't understand. No one ever did.

But she had a point on this note. "If anything changes, you will call me."

"Alex—"

"You *will* call me."

She sighed. "Yes, fine, if anything suddenly goes sideways, I'll find a way to get a hold of you."

He shouldn't take her word for it. In fact, he should be packing right now. But Alex found himself saying, "Okay."

"Goodbye, Alex."

"Bye." He hung up just as Kendall opened the bathroom door. She hesitated, as if the few feet between the door and the bed were too much when they'd both been wrapped up in each other all night. But she seemed to steel herself and padded naked to the bed. "Give me two," he said.

"Sure."

His misgivings didn't disappear as he brushed his teeth. Alex half hoped that Kendall would be gone when he finished and make the choice for him, but he couldn't ignore the relief at seeing her sitting so primly on his bed. He grinned. "Morning."

"Morning." She gave him a smile of her own. "You had to call out for work?"

"Yeah, I own a bar in Dawson's Creek."

Her eyes went wide. "Dawson's...Creek."

"Yeah, I know. It's ridiculous and the locals get a kick out of it, but we precede that TV show."

Kendall grinned. "Cool."

"I sort of unofficially inherited it when my grandfather retired and moved to Mexico a few years back." Though, truth be told, he'd run the business for longer than that. As Pop used to be so fond of reminding him, he wasn't a young man anymore. He'd taught Alex everything he knew about running the place, and the business degree had filled in the gaps.

Kendall tucked the sheet around her and gave him her full attention. "Tell me about it."

This wasn't part of the plan. Sex, yes, but making small talk? Alex still found himself climbing into bed next to her and reclining against the pillows. "When I was a kid, it was pure dive bar. The kind of place where people drink themselves stupid and brawl when the night goes on too long." He grinned. "But most of my good memories from childhood are wrapped up in that building. The cigarette smoke that seemed to permeate everything. The sticky bar. The rolling laughter of good-natured ribbing between men who had been friends longer than I'd been alive. And, through it all, Pop held the center, as steady as gravity."

"Sounds like an interesting place."

He laughed at her dubious expression. "When I took over managing it, I started shifting things around. We still get the regulars during the day, but it's more of a hipster kind of place in the evening with fancy drinks and tiny food." The regulars had a special menu that wasn't available to anyone else, because he'd be damned before he drove them out while he worked at elevating the place. They might bitch about the laws against smoking inside now, but they still showed up like clockwork.

"Fancy drinks and tiny food." Kendall tilted her head to the side. "I can't see it. You're not really the fancy drinks and tiny food kind of guy."

"You think so?" He tugged gently on a strand of her hair. "How would you know?"

She opened her mouth, but seemed to reconsider what she'd been about to say. "That's fair. I'm afraid I've made some assumptions about you from the beginning that weren't very flattering—or true."

Her words stung a little, but they had no reason to. She wasn't the first person who'd looked at him and thought that he was trouble. Good for one thing or another, but not the kind of guy a woman kept around for longer than a few nights. Not the kind they saw themselves walking down the aisle to or raising a family with. He forced a laugh. "You aren't the first."

"Doesn't make it right." She worried her bottom lip. "You've been nothing but amazing to me, and honestly I don't deserve it."

That wasn't the truth. "Sweetheart, why wouldn't you deserve it?"

"Because I was so rude to you. Seriously rude. And then..." She shook her head. "I suppose it doesn't matter now. But for what it's worth, I'm sorry."

Alex laced his fingers through hers and brought their linked hands up to kiss her knuckles. "What do you do?"

"I'm the assistant sales manager for a trio of hotels in New York." She made a face. "It's the same job I've had pretty much since I got out of college. I should have seen more upward movement at this point, but I keep getting passed over for promotions."

They'd gotten unexpectedly heavy for so early in the morning. He should turn the conversation to lighter things, but he didn't like the way her expression fell when she talked about work. "Do you like the job?"

"Yes. I mean, most days aren't totally terrible. I like dealing with the long-term contracts and the satisfaction of knowing that my work is helping the bottom line." She shrugged. "I just feel... stagnant. Like somewhere along the line, I got into a rut without realizing it and now I don't know what I'm supposed to do about it."

He couldn't fix her life. It wasn't his job to even try. That wasn't the role he was meant to play in her life. But they had the next six days, and he could leave her better than he'd found her. "I have just the distraction."

Her lips curved. "That's one hell of a line."

"Is it a line if it's the truth?" He tugged on her hand, and she allowed him to urge her up to straddle him.

Kendall laughed, the lingering tension dissipating as she settled against him, "No, I don't suppose it is."

* * *

KENDALL NEVER WOULD HAVE CONSIDERED herself sex-crazed, but after spending the day in Alex's bed, she feared the term fit. Every time she started to feel awkward about staying so long, or wonder if she should leave, he'd slide a hand between her thighs or move down her body, trailing kisses in his wake, and she'd put off going back to her room for a little while longer.

Now, she wasn't sure she was physically capable of walking away.

Alex kissed the back of her neck as he pumped slowly into her. "You hungry, sweetheart?" He cupped her breast with one hand and pressed his other to her clit. Not circling. She was far too sensitive for that kind of stimulation at this point. But the light pressure as he fucked her slowly has her rising in a steady wave of pleasure.

She leaned back against him, letting him control this fully. "I can't believe you're asking me that right now."

"Mmm." He pressed another kiss to her neck. "Once more and we can go find food."

Kendall gave a desperate laugh. "You're bargaining orgasms for food right now."

"Yeah." Totally unrepentant, and she adored that about him. He didn't pick up his pace, though. He just kept that low, languid movement as if he was enjoying drawing this out as much as she was.

She never wanted it to end.

Her body hadn't gotten the memo, though. Her orgasm rolled through her in a soft wave that had her writhing against him. Alex flipped her onto her stomach and drove into her, desire turning them into desperate creatures. More, more, always more.

If this fling didn't have a built-in expiration date, it might scare the hell out of her.

It took long minutes before their breathing settled back into something resembling normal. Kendall rolled to face him, and Alex immediately pulled her close. "So, about that food."

She laughed against his chest. "I really don't know if my legs will hold me after today."

"That's fine. I'll hold both of us."

How could he *say* things like that with a straight face? As if he wasn't shaking her world right down to the very bedrock of her existence. She cuddled closer and pressed a kiss to the center of his chest. "In that case, food would be most welcome."

They parted just long enough to shower and change. Through it all, Kendall kept wondering if she'd imagined the whole night in some kind of fever dream. Surely this wasn't real. Surely she hadn't thrown caution to the wind in the most dramatic way possible and fallen into bed with the sexiest man she'd ever met.

Surely she hadn't had semi-public sex and a *very* public orgasm.

But when she opened her door, there Alex was. He grinned at the sight of her, as if she'd just delivered the best present and he couldn't wait to open it. "I like the dress."

She looked down at the dress in question. Floral, again. She hadn't realized how much floral she owned until this trip. Too much, probably. Kendall smoothed down the fabric and returned his smile. "Thanks."

His blue eyes went intense for a moment. "I'm not going to ask what you're wearing under it."

"Okay," she said slowly.

"Because if I find out you're pulling a repeat of last night, we're not going to make it far enough from your room to get that food I promised you." He caught her hips and pulled her a step into the hallway, waiting for the door to shut completely before he tucked her under his arm and pointed them in the direction of the dining room. They walked together as if they'd done this a thousand times before.

As if they fit.

No, she couldn't think about that. Even if they somehow thought to extend this past the end of the trip, she lived in a completely different state. He obviously had deep roots in his town. She had a job that needed her, even if it frustrated her on a daily basis. Moving across the country for a man she just met...

What was she even thinking? Alex hadn't promised her anything but right now. Stressing about a what-if scenario that would never happen was what she did when she wasn't on vacation. What her sisters had teased her for ever since she was a kid. She wasn't that woman right now. She refused to be.

They stopped just inside the room and she froze. All her friends except Aubrey sat around a table. Was she supposed to walk over there with Alex? It would invite questions she didn't know how to answer, and put both of them on the spot. She glanced up to ask him... she wasn't sure what, but she stopped when she noticed him looking at something intensely. "What's wrong?"

"Nothing." He gave himself a shake and smiled down at her. "I was just thinking I'm not in the mood for my friend to give me shit."

Relief crashed over her, almost swallowing the pinprick of guilt. "Me, too."

"Want to just grab a table over here?"

The coward's way out, maybe, but she still wasn't ready to face her friends on multiple different levels. "Please." She clung to his hand as he led her to a table with a few free seats in the opposite direction of their friends. The guilt wouldn't quite leave, though. Kendall cleared her throat. "I'm not ashamed of you. That's not why I didn't want to go over there."

Alex held out her chair and waited for her to sit before he sank into the chair next to her. "I know."

She started to change the subject, but stopped "I don't even think they'd pepper us with a bunch of questions or anything. Maybe back in college, but I'd like to think we're beyond that now." She hesitated, but he just watched her with those serious blue eyes and she found herself talking freely. "Though maybe that's because we're not as close as we used to be."

"Am I keeping you from them?"

She shook her head. "No. Honestly, you're probably saving them from *me*. All everyone wanted to do on this vacation is relax, and if left to my own devices, I'll have us planned down to the last minute." She waved a vague hand. "It makes me feel more in control to have a plan."

"Aw, sweetheart." He took her hand and gave it a squeeze. "You seem to be doing just fine without a plan."

"Yeah, I guess I am." She managed a smile. "Honestly, I probably should have dragged my sisters on this cruise, too. Well, not Gretchen. She's living in happily married bliss, and I doubt my brother-in-law would appreciate my taking her on a singles' cruise."

"What are you sisters like?"

"Totally different from me." She laughed, thinking of them. Grams always called them three peas in a pod, and she might seem them that way, but no one else did. "Gretchen is about as perfect as a person can be. She's strong and stubborn and always knows exactly where she's headed. Marley is the exact opposite. Anything resembling long-term commitment makes her break out in hives. I don't think she's stayed in one place longer than a year since she graduated high school."

Alex grinned. "They sound cool, but I definitely prefer you."

His easy words warmed her right down to her soul, even as a little voice in the back of her mind whispered not to make this into something it wasn't. They were indulging in a vacation fling. End of story.

Right?

CHAPTER 9

*K*endall didn't mean to stay the night in Alex's room. She really didn't. But somehow dawn came and she was naked and wrapped up with him. Again. She blinked into the low light of the room, an unfamiliar panic squeezing her chest. It was too easy being with him. Too perfect. He respected her boundaries, didn't think she was uptight and a bore, and was beyond amazing in bed. Rationally, she knew this was what a vacation fling could be. No drama. No complications. Just pure fun and bliss.

It didn't change the fact that she could only turn off her brain for so long. It felt like every single doubt and insecurity and worry she *should* have had over the last couple days decided in that moment to create an avalanche designed to bury her.

What was she *doing?*

She'd dragged her friends on this cruise, ended up providing them with the *opposite* experience she'd promised, and then promptly abandoned them to ride the cock of a near-stranger. Oh, Alex didn't feel like a stranger any longer, but that didn't change the fact that she'd only known him a few days and she'd known her friends over a decade at this point. It shouldn't have been a tough decision on who she spent her time with.

She had to get out of here now, while Alex still slept, or she'd forget all about her duty to her friends and spend the rest of the day in bed with him. Again.

God, she was the worst friend ever.

Kendall carefully slipped out from beneath Alex's arm and then climbed off the bed. She hesitated and, even though she knew better, she looked back. The sight of him caused something in her chest to clang uncomfortably. He was so attractive even while asleep, all lean strength and a surprising vulnerability. Without those blue eyes seeming to read her thoughts, he looked younger, less world-weary. It made her want to climb back into bed, to tease the covers down past his hips, to take him in her mouth and...

No.

No.

She spun around and closed her eyes. She could do this. She just had to walk away. They'd probably see each other again—Kendall didn't think she could keep from seeking him out—but she had other priorities to see to right now. She yanked on her dress and slipped into her sandals. At last moment, she doubled back and scrawled him a quick note on a pad of paper next to the bed. There. That would help, right? She hoped so.

As she stepped out into the hallway, she froze at the sight of a familiar person edging into the hallway with the same furtive movements Kendall currently enacted. Benjamin. Their eyes met over the short distance between Alex's room and the one he'd just left... the next door down. *Is that Alex's friend's room?* No way to know without asking, and the deer-in-headlights look on Benjamin's face discouraged any kind of questioning. So she tried for a neutral expression and gave a little wave.

They walked side by side back to their cabins and it wasn't until Kendall had her hand on her doorknob that Benjamin spoke. "Thanks for this trip, Kendall. I know it's not what you planned, but I think it's good for us. All of us."

"Me, too." She didn't know what else to say. She and Benjamin had been friends for a long time, but it wasn't the kind of friendship where they shared dirty details about sexual exploits. Part of that was because Kendall never *had* dirty details to share before now. She tried for a smile. "See you on the excursion today?"

"Yeah, maybe."

Easy enough to read between the lines there. Yeah, he'd be there, if his hookup didn't entail doing something else the same way hers had yesterday. Her skin went hot and she pushed through the door and shut it softly behind her. There were hours yet before they needed to report to the deck for the excursion into Cocoa Bay, so she'd be smart to get some sleep.

Except when she laid down, her brain refused to settle. Instead, it kept flashing memories from the last two days with Alex. His voice in her ear, encouraging her to tell him exactly what she wanted so he could give it to her. His hands and mouth on her, driving her pleasure to new heights. The way he watched her when she rode his cock, as if he couldn't believe this was happening any more than she could.

As if he wanted to memorize every moment.

Maybe she should have stayed in his bed a little longer before she rushed off. Now that she had a little distance from him, she felt silly for bolting. It wasn't like he planned on chaining her to his bed. She shivered. Though that wasn't an entirely unpleasant thought.

To distract herself, she showered and took her time

getting ready. Kendall hesitated in front of her suitcase. She'd bought the bright pink bikini on a whim, but it covered far less than the others she owned, and she'd never worked up the courage to wear it. She wasn't even sure why she'd packed it at all.

She picked up the suit and pressed her lips together. If ever there was a time to wear this suit, it was now, while she still rode the high from Alex's presence. Imagining his reaction to seeing her in it was enough to have her pulling the suit on and adjusting it as much as she could. She pulled her wrap around herself, still feeling downright decadent, and opened her door.

Grace stood there, her hands on her hips. "Oh good. You're not dead."

"Um, what?"

"Kendall, you've been missing in action for twenty-four hours. If I hadn't seen you leaving dinner last night, I would have organized a search party." She cast a critical glance over Kendall. "You look good. Glowy."

Now that she mentioned it, Grace did, too. Kendall frowned. "Is that a *hickey?*"

"What? No. Of course not." Grace pulled at her top as if that would make a difference. "We're not talking about me right now."

"Um, maybe we should be." Kendall propped her hands on her hips. "You found a vacation hook-up!"

"No, it's not like that." But Grace was *blushing*. "I'm just playing a game."

"Whatever you want to call it."

"Kendall!"

She held up her hands. "Sure, sure, I'm supportive. This is me being supportive of your 'game.'" She grinned. "Are you doing the day trip today?"

"That's what I came to ask you. The others are around."

She waved a hand vaguely at the other cabins. "They all seem to be enjoying themselves."

"Some more than others," Kendall murmured. She wasn't about to gossip about Benjamin, but the questions about him and Alex's friend burned the inside of her lips. Not her business. It *so* wasn't her business. She'd just keep the whole thing to herself.

"You never answered my question. Where have you been?"

"There's a guy," she started, but stalled out almost as soon as she'd begun. How could she explain to Grace what being with Alex felt like? She and Grace had always been really similar in how they approached certain things; it was part of the reason they'd stayed close over the years. Kendall lifted her hands and let them fall.

"The bathroom guy?"

"Yeah." She laughed. "He makes me feel like I don't have any responsibilities. Like that's okay."

"I think I understand." A strange expression flickered over Grace's face before she gave a tight smile. "How about breakfast?"

"That would be great." Even though she hadn't really planned to seek Alex out, not yet, she couldn't help the thread of disappointment that twined through her as she fell into step next to her friend. It was only day four. There were still four days left to spend however she chose. She'd be an idiot if she spent the entire cruise locked in a bedroom with a man, no matter how sexy he was.

But as she and Grace sat down and ate, she couldn't help looking for him. It was crazy, simply unhinged. He was just a man who, while being a whole cut above the rest, really was only a vacation fling. That was it. That's all it could be.

Right?

"Grace?"

Her friend stopped mid-bite, her attention narrowing on Kendall. "Yes?"

She spoke before she could stop herself, her words tumbling over themselves to escape her lips. "Do you think it's possible for a long-distance relationship that started as a fling to work?"

There it was again, that strange look on her friend's face that she'd never seen before. "There's a lot of technological options that can close the distance these days. And plane trips aren't that expensive. So… Yes, I think a long-distance relationship could work."

"That sounds very logical and I don't feel very logical right now." Kendall sat back. She didn't know if that made her feel better or worse. All Alex had promised her was good sex that she asked for. Yes, they'd spent quite a bit of time talking in between rounds of orgasms, but that just meant he wasn't a monster. It didn't mean he was *interested*.

Surely she wasn't thinking about asking Alex to give this a go…right?

* * *

ALEX WOKE UP ALONE. He should have known it would happen. Things were going too good with Kendall. Hell, he should thank her for putting the brakes on and creating some distance between them. Except he didn't feel like thanking her. He wanted to search the ship until he found her and demand to know why she hadn't woken him up to say goodbye.

He sat up and got distracted by a crinkle. Alex frowned at the piece of paper neatly folded on the pillow Kendall hadn't managed to use last night. She'd been too busy wrapping around him like a friendly octopus. Not that he minded. He couldn't remember the last time he'd literally slept with someone. His partners were usually too busy bending over backward to tell him that they knew this was no strings attached and they didn't expect anything of him.

It had never bothered Alex before.

Now, he looked at the note Kendall left like it was a bomb just waiting to go off. It could be anything. A compilation of words meant to let him down easy. A fucking thank you for the sex. With Kendall, he couldn't be sure. Honestly, he should be relieved. After the last couple days, he was already entangled in her. Getting more so was a mistake. He'd learned that lesson too many times before. First with his parents, then later on in the relationships he'd naively thought were going to go the distance. They never did.

Eventually, everyone left.

Even as he told himself to just toss the note in the trash, he carefully picked it up and unfolded it. Even her fucking scrawl was cute. He blinked, waiting for the words to conform to expectations. Instead, what he read veered in the opposite direction.

I have to run before my friends think I totally abandoned them... See you tonight?

Her excuse felt flat, but he didn't begrudge her it. She was right—they needed some space, no matter how much he resented the distance. Fuck. What was he *doing?* He'd never had to worry about this kind of thing before, and now he was neck deep and sinking fast. All because of Kendall and her fledgling confidence and vaguely neurotic ways.

Alex dragged his hands over his face. Shower and food and a conversation with Lucas, if he could snag him. Alex had done some abandoning of his own on this cruise and, though he'd fully intended to *really* abandon the ship, it didn't make him less of a jackass for doing it. Though Lucas was more than capable of hunting him down if he needed something, it didn't make Alex's actions any less shitty.

Fifteen minutes later, he knocked on Lucas's door. His friend answered, looking more relaxed than he'd seen him in recent memory. "Hey, stranger."

"Hey stranger, yourself." He motioned vaguely down the hallway. "You going on the excursion today?"

"Nah." Lucas gave a slow grin that lit up his eyes. "I have plans."

"Plans," Alex echoed. "So much for not taking advantage of the party cruise."

"You're one to throw stones." Luca laughed. "You've got freshly-fucked written all over you." He shook his head. "We can plan to meet up for drinks later, or…"

"No, no, don't let me distract you from your vacation fling." Having Lucas focused elsewhere meant Alex didn't have the distraction *he* was hoping for, but he couldn't begrudge his friend whatever joy he'd found on this cruise. "I'm going to spend the day relaxing."

Which was how Alex found himself in Cocoa Beach instead of doing literally anything else. He moved with the group he'd accidentally joined, his hands in his pockets, feeling a bit like a kindergartener. The idea of a water park or all the other activities they offered didn't appeal, so he ended up on the "chill" side of the island, surveying a long beach with cabanas, lounge chairs, and other shit like that set up.

Though Alex could barely look at the lounge chairs without thinking about Kendall riding his cock on one the other night. He clenched his jaw and adjusted his shorts. Relaxation. Right. Somehow, it had seemed like a good enough idea when he mentioned it, but now he had a full day laid out ahead of him and he was supposed to… sun himself?

What the fuck was he even doing here?

A flash of pink farther down the beach caught his eye and Alex went still. Even at this distance, he *knew* that body, had kissed his way along the curve of her waist, had gripped her lithe thighs, had buried his face in her now-barely-concealed pussy. Kendall.

He started for her without having any intention of doing so. With each step, more details came into focus. The bright pink bikini that stood out against her pale skin. How *little* those scraps of fabric covered. The curves of her ass were mostly left bare, the suit cutting up in almost a V to its ties. She turned to say something to the pretty Asian woman next to her and he got a good look at the front of it.

Fuck.

The suit dipped so low in the front, he could *almost* see her pussy. And the top's triangles looked in danger of sliding out of place with one wrong move. He simultaneously wanted to throw a towel over her and fall to his knees and worship her right here and now.

He should stop. Should turn around. Should walk away until he had control of himself, until he was sure he could act right in an interaction with her.

Alex didn't do any of those things. He marched up to her, stepping between her and the sun, and growled. "You didn't say goodbye this morning."

"Ah!" Kendall jumped and, Jesus, he thought he might have to lunge forward to cover her breasts from a wardrobe malfunction before anyone saw. Thankfully—wretchedly—the fabric stayed in place. She took a step back and her hands fluttered at her sides. "Oh. Alex. It's you."

He had absolutely no reason to be annoyed at her response. None at all. But he couldn't help wanting some fucking acknowledgement. Something to indicate she was as messed up over him as he was over her. He turned to her friend and held out a hand. "We didn't meet properly before. I'm Alex."

"Grace," she said slowly and gave him a solid handshake.

"Need some help setting up?"

She looked between them and arched her eyebrows. "Actually, I think I'm going to find a drink. I'll be back... in fifteen minutes or so."

"Traitor," Kendall hissed.

And, yeah, that annoyed the shit out of Alex. First she snuck out, leaving that vague ass note, and now she obviously didn't want to be alone with him. He started to say it was fine, that *he'd* leave, but Grace was gone before he had a chance, her confident stride creating distance between them quickly. He turned back to Kendall and crossed his arms over his chest. "You left."

"I left you a note." She looked around like she expected an audience to gather, but no one was paying them the least bit of attention. "I'm trying to be reasonable."

This should be good. "Reasonable."

"Yes, *reasonable*. I booked this trip to reconnect with friends, and I've spent most of the time with you." She propped her hands on her hips, and it was everything he could do to keep his gaze on her face. "Look, at the end of this you're going back to Dawson's Creek and I'm going back to New York, and while that is good and fine and whatever, I like being with you a lot and I needed some distance to get my head on straight."

Because she was falling for him.

Just like he was falling for her.

The realization should send him running for the hills. He knew what came after that initial blissful time. Reality. Shit would happen, life would worm its way through the cracks, and she'd realize this was all a mistake and leave. Then he'd be left picking up the pieces yet again. There were no guarantees in the future, nothing except the simple truth that the wheel always turned and it always sent people he cared about scattering before it. Away from him.

Even as he laid out all the reasons he should turn around and walk away, Alex planted his feet. "Did it work?"

She blinked. "Did what work?"

"The distance. Did it get your head on straight?" He stepped closer and lowered his voice. "Or did you pick out that bikini hoping I'd see you in it and lose my fucking mind?"

She tugged at the ties of her bottoms, as if that would do a damn thing to cover her more. "I bought this before I knew you."

That, he believed. "Did you wear it before today?"

Her blush told him all he needed to know, but he wanted verbal confirmation, too. Finally, Kendall gave a jerky shake of her head. "No, I've never worn it before." She didn't quite look him in the face. "I was feeling good and confident so I put it on."

Being around this woman was like watching a flower bloom in real time. He had no illusions; he wasn't the cause, not really. He was just the tool at hand she used to facilitate the growth. What a fucking privilege to play that role. He took another step closer. "And how do you feel right now while you're wearing it?"

"Really good," she breathed. "I feel absolutely indecent."

"You look indecent." He couldn't help the rough edge in his voice. He didn't want to. "I thought you were a nice girl, sweetheart, but you sure as hell seem intent on tormenting me."

Her lips curved. "I am a nice girl."

"Mmhmm." He didn't touch her. He didn't trust himself to go that far when they stood in the middle of a beach full of people. "So nice you're about to get a lump of coal for Christmas."

She laughed. "Strangely enough, I'm not even sorry." Kendall trailed a single finger down his chest, tracing the faint line of his muscles. "How do you feel about hammocks?"

Alex blinked. "What?"

"I saw some advertised, but I think they're a little back from the beach in the shade." She gave another of those small, secret smiles. "I haven't been on a hammock since I was a kid. Might be just the kind of experience this vacation needs."

He caught her hand, but forced his feet still. "What about your friend?"

"Grace has an agenda for today, so she was going to be abandoning me before too long anyways." She hesitated. "But you're right. I should let her know." She gripped his hand and dragged him behind her to the bar where her friend had posted up. The woman gave them a significant look, but just shook her head as Kendall rattled off some excuse and then hauled Alex behind her toward the hammocks scattered just inside the tree line. They weren't exactly private, but it seemed most people had gravitated to the beach and the bar, so the area surrounding them was mostly deserted.

Kendall stopped in front of one, but Alex didn't. He scooped her into his arms and turned around to sink carefully onto the network of interlaced rope. It gave beneath their weight, folding around them so they were cradled in it. "There." He held still while she shifted so she could face him. "You have me in a hammock, sweetheart. Now what are you going to do with me?"

CHAPTER 10

*T*his wasn't part of the plan, but in that moment, Kendall decided that it didn't matter. She had Alex for now and that had to be enough. Who cared if it didn't check any boxes or make any kind of logical sense? She enjoyed every moment she spent with him, and she couldn't say that about much else in her life these days.

She laced her fingers through the hammock and used the hold to pull herself a little higher on Alex's body until they were lined up perfectly. The give of the rope made it nearly impossible to straddle him effectively, but she made do. "Well, first thing's first. I'm going to kiss you." She waited a beat for him to nod and then did exactly that. It started out light and almost sweet, but she ached too much to let it stay there.

Because Alex was right. This swimsuit, knowing he saw her in it and wanted her... It had her so twisted up, she might explode if she didn't get relief soon. If she didn't get *him* soon.

He coasted his hands up her sides and urged her back a little. "I have to—" He used his thumbs to tug her top to either side, baring her breasts. "Christ, Kendall." He sounded like he was in complete agony because of *her*, because he wanted her so desperately.

She wanted him just as much. She felt crazed with it. Kendall kissed him again, dragging her breasts against his chest. It felt wicked. So incredibly wicked. The sensation was only heightened when Alex slid his hand down her spine and into her bottoms, reaching to push a single finger into her from behind. "Oh!"

"I can't get enough of you." He dragged her higher on his chest and pushed a second finger into her. The new position allowed him access to her breasts and he wasted no time capturing one nipple and sucking hard. "You're like a drug I don't want to quit."

"I feel the same way," she gasped. It was because of that vacation sex. It had to be. Surely she couldn't possibly feel this strongly for a man she'd just met, no matter how skilled he was at coaxing orgasms from her.

The hammock twisted, but she didn't care. She didn't care about anything but the way he made her feel. "I was supposed to get distance from you."

Alex leaned back enough to meet her gaze even as he kept fucking her slowly, thoroughly with his fingers. "Do you still want space, sweetheart?"

"No," she breathed. It took two tries to concentrate enough to keep speaking. "I want you to make me come..." She licked her lips. "And then I want to suck your cock."

His body went tight and still against hers. "What the lady wants, the lady gets." He towed her back down to claim her mouth and then slipped his free hand between them to tug her bottoms to the side so he had access to her clit. Alex surrounded her, overwhelmed her, claimed her, and she couldn't do anything but writhe against him as she kissed him with everything she had. Speaking words that had no business being voiced.

Yes, yes, yes.

Don't stop.

Please don't ever stop.

Even as part of her wanted to hold out, even after such a short time, Alex already knew her body too well. She came with a cry that he kissed from her lips and then he gentled his touch, bringing her back down to earth. It took the edge off, but only barely. And, this time, she wasn't leaving him high and dry.

Kendall ended up needing his help to climb out of the hammock safely, and Alex kept himself between her and the rest of the beach as she adjusted her swimsuit with shaking hands. It felt even more indecent than it had when she put it on this morning. Her blood pounded through her body with each heartbeat. Demanding more. Needing him.

She urged Alex back onto the hammock, but this time sitting sideways so his feet rested on the ground. Kendall sank to her knees in front of him and licked her lips. "I've been thinking about this a lot."

"Oh yeah?" His voice came out strained and knowing *she* was the reason made her shiver.

"Yeah." She hooked her fingers into the top of his swim trunks and worked them down far enough to free his cock. As she dipped down, Alex sank his hands into her hair and gathered it up away from her face. Giving her free range of motion. Giving him a clear view of everything she planned on doing.

She gave him a cautious stroke, but she was too impatient. Kendall licked her lips again and flicked her tongue out to taste him. He was so warm and smooth and hard and... Yeah, she needed more. She gave up on teasing and sucked him down hard, earning a strangled curse from Alex. His obviously fracturing control only made her needier, and so she gave herself over to sucking his cock. Her world narrowed down to the warm sand beneath her knees, to the coiled muscles of his thighs against her hands as he fought to hold still, to swallowing down as much of his hard length as she could. Over and over again.

His grip tightened in her hair. "Sweetheart, you keep doing that and I'm going to come."

Good. She recognized the warning, though. Kendall forced herself to slow down and lift her head. *Say what you want and I'll give it to you.* She gave him another lick. "Come in my mouth, Alex."

"Fuck," he growled. "You sure?"

"Yes." She didn't give him a chance to argue further. Kendall resumed her pace, sucking him down deep and withdrawing almost all the way, only to repeat the action. His hips began moving the slightest bit, rising to meet her descent, as if he couldn't help himself. She loved that. She loved the exact moment his control splintered, loved what came next. And then he was coming in great spurts that she eagerly drank down.

"That's right, sweetheart. Suck me, Kendall. *Fuck.*" His fingers became a gentle cage around her head as he finished, and Kendall had never felt more powerful than she did in the moment she looked up and found him staring dazedly at her.

It didn't last long.

Alex's brows slammed down and he hauled her to her feet. She started to protest but he laid a kiss on her lips and then turned around to push her into the same position he'd just occupied. Half a second to shove his cock back into his swim trunks and then *he* was on his knees. Kendall started to sit up, but he pressed a hand flat against her stomach, stopping her. "I'm not done."

She should stop this now. She'd come. He'd come. They

should… She didn't know. Something. But Kendall's blood heated at the way Alex's gaze raked over her possessively. He pulled at the strings on one side of her bottoms, undoing it. A tug and he bared her pussy.

Suddenly Kendall didn't care if anyone saw them. The fact that they were close enough to hear people partying on the beach only made it hotter as Alex wedged his hands beneath her ass and dragged his tongue over her as if savoring her taste. She laced her fingers through his hair and arched up to meet his mouth. "Anyone could walk over."

"Yeah," he rumbled against her clit. "And they'd think I'm the luckiest bastard in the world to get to taste your sweet pussy."

She moaned. "*Alex.*"

"Would you make me stop?"

It took her several long seconds to understand the question. "If someone sees us?"

He held her gaze as he gave her pussy another long lick. "Yeah. If they walked up, would you make me stop?"

"No." She spread her legs wider. "No, I wouldn't. I don't want you to ever stop."

"I won't. Not until you come for me again."

And then there was no more talking. He drove her pleasure higher with a ruthlessness Alex had never displayed before. Kendall could do nothing but cling to him and the hammock and let him take her for this ride. He shoved her into an orgasm that bowed her back and had her clamping her hand over her mouth to keep from crying out. Too good. Everything with him was *too good*. It defied explanation.

He rested his forehead against her stomach, breathing just as hard as she was. "Have dinner with me."

She blinked up at the sunlight filtering through the trees overhead. "I had dinner with you last night."

"I don't mean like that. I mean…" He took a slow inhale

and an even slower exhale. "Considering our circumstances, it seems weird as shit to ask you out on a date, but that's what I'm doing."

A date.

Now was the time to reestablish boundaries, to remind them both that this could never last past the point when the ship docked in New York again. That the only reasonable and realistic outcome ended with them back in their respective lives with absolutely no overlap. That even trying long distance just set them both up for angst and heartbreak.

There was only one problem.

She didn't feel like being reasonable right now. She wanted the fantasy Alex wove around her. More, she wanted time with him. All the time with him she could possibly have. "Yes. I'd love to have a date with you."

He carefully retied her swimsuit bottoms and held out a hand. "Let's start now."

* * *

ALEX WASN'T sure what he intended when he told Kendall they'd start their date now, but he hadn't expected to end up on a pair of kayaks out in the water inside of twenty minutes. It wasn't that he had a problem with water. He didn't. He just had a problem with all the shit that lived in water. But she'd grinned at him and he'd been completely incapable of saying no.

"What's your grandfather like?"

He paddled steadily, keeping pace with her as she sent her kayak coasting across the top of the water. "He's a cranky old bastard, but he's one of the best men I've ever known." Alex could just leave it at that, but he found himself elaborating. "My parents weren't a good match. Shouldn't have been together. Sure as fuck shouldn't have procreated. Their marriage imploded when I was a kid and my mom took off right after. My dad lasted until I was thirteen, but he never planned on staying in Dawson's Creek. Pop is *his* dad and he took me in. It wasn't easy on either of us, but we figured it out eventually."

He very carefully didn't look at her. Pity was the last thing he wanted, and Kendall had too good a heart not to feel it for the kid he'd been. Abandoned by *both* his parents. If it wasn't for Pop, Alex would have ended up on a bad road, a thousand times worse than the wild years he'd had while he was acting out. At least he'd had a safety net in place. A lot of kids who shared similar situations didn't even have that.

"My parents died when I was nine."

That got his attention. They both stopped paddling and he finally looked at her. No pity in those green eyes. Just a deep understanding, a shared trauma. "I'm sorry."

"I ended up in a similar situation to you—my grandmother took over. And I had my sisters even if none of us ever quite fit into the small town I grew up in. Except maybe Gretchen. I think she could fit in anywhere. She's one of those stories that shouldn't be real. Still in love with her high school sweetheart after nearly fifteen years, married for ten of them."

There were times when he was younger when he would have killed to have a sibling. Someone who lived through the same shit, someone who would have his back no matter what. It wasn't until Alex got older that he realized not all sibling relationships were healthy. He'd survived and flourished despite his background. If there were more of them, no telling if his theoretical siblings would have done the same.

No, it was better that he was alone. Simpler.

That didn't stop him from being so fucking grateful to find out that Kendall *wasn't* alone. "Your sister sounds great."

"She is." She sighed. "Honestly, it's a little annoying. She created this standard that neither me nor Marley could ever quite live up to. It didn't stop me from trying. But my little sister is what you'd call a wild child."

He grinned. "I'm familiar with the concept."

"I bet you are." She dipped her fingers into the ocean and flicked a few drops of water in his direction. "You were one, weren't you?"

"Guilty." He set his paddle over his knees and leaned forward, enjoying this moment. "It's honestly kind of embarrassing how much of a cliché I was. All anger and hormones and a self-destructive tendency that almost landed me in juvie at one point."

Her smile turned a little sad. "You turned it around."

"Pop turned me around. Pop and the bar. He gave me a safe space to fuck up, and then grounded me for like six months and made me work the bar as punishment." Alex snorted. "I thought it was hell on earth, but in hindsight he was teaching me a lot. Giving me a foundation that would see me through."

"Buildings don't leave you," she murmured.

Her words hit a little too close to home. He forced a laugh. "What about you? Your older sister was a paragon. You little sister was the wild child. You never really told me where you fit into that."

"Isn't it obvious?" Again, that twist of her lips that wasn't quite a smile. "I'm the one who never steps out of line, who ended up with an over-developed sense of responsibility." She picked up her paddle and then set it down again over her knees. "My grandmother was a strong personality—strong enough to keep all of us in line even though she lost her daughter the same way we lost our mom. But she had her hands full. I don't know when I decided that I would be the one not to cause her any grief, but that's where I ended up. I never got into trouble. I never broke the rules. I worked my ass off to get into a decent college that also wouldn't break the bank." She made a motion like she was checking off boxes in a list. "I didn't want to be a burden."

He understood that, even if he'd never leaned in that direction with Pop. "We're a boatload of issues."

"You can say that again." This time, her smile seemed more genuine. "I've been in therapy since I was old enough to realize it would help, but I'm still a work in progress."

"We all are."

She shifted her grip on her paddle. "Alex?"

This was where she let him down gently. Where she said that this was fun, but that's all it was. He knew this couldn't go anywhere. Fuck, he knew it better than anyone. That hadn't stopped him from crossing the lines they'd created time and time again. He'd asked her on a goddamn date.

He'd had a few girlfriends. Back when he was in his early twenties and still hadn't realized the exact mold life had shoved him into. When part of him still thought he might end up with a future like the ones meant for other people. Women loved him... within certain boundaries. He was good enough to fuck, good enough to play around with for a short-term fling, but he wasn't husband material. After being told that for the third fucking time by a woman he thought was falling for him the same way he was falling for her? Yeah, Alex stopped trying to change other people's perception of him. Better to just lay out expectations right at the beginning and let everyone walk away with their hearts unbruised.

He braced himself to have this conversation yet again. "Yeah?"

"This has been really, really nice." She tucked her wind-blown hair back behind her ears. "I thought this trip was going to be a disaster and, because of you, it's been some of the best days in living memory for me."

But that's all it is.

She took a deep breath. "I don't want it to end."

He blinked. "What?"

"I..." Another of those deep, fortifying breaths. "I don't want it to end. I'll admit that I haven't had a ton of time for dating and that kind of thing—and I guess I still don't—but surely this connection isn't only because we're having hot vacation sex?" She kept fidgeting, adjusting her swimsuit, touching the paddle, fixing her hair again. "I mean, maybe I'm reading too much into it."

Holy shit, she wasn't letting him down gently.

Shock made him slow to respond. He could barely hear his words over the buzzing in his ears. "You don't want this to end."

"Oh god, I misread things, didn't I?" She picked up her paddle. "Forget I said anything."

"Wait." He reached out and laid a hand over hers, holding her in place. "Just give me a damn minute. I thought you were going to say you'd had your fun and it was over now. It's taking me a second to catch up."

"Over now?" Kendall gave a rough laugh. "I don't know what you were thinking when you were in that hammock with me, but I meant it when I said I can't get enough of you. Like I said—"

"I feel the same way," he blurted. "This isn't normal for me, either." Something flared in his chest, hot and uncomfortable and hopeful. He laced his fingers through hers. "I'm not ready for this to end."

He hesitated, wondering if the universe would choose that moment to slap him down for daring speak that shit. It always had in the past. But nothing happened. No shark fin circled them. No tidal wave appeared to sweep them under. Kendall didn't suddenly declare that she'd changed her mind and never wanted to see him again. He let out a slow breath.

"You really thought I'd say I was done with this?" She sounded so incredulous, he almost laughed.

Alex shrugged, though the move felt too tense to really pull off. "It's happened before."

She frowned, but then her expression cleared as understanding dawned. "They were idiots."

Now, he did laugh. "They didn't feel the same way." Not after they'd gotten to walk on the wild side with him. He wasn't that guy anymore, but some scars never quite healed right. He just hadn't realized how raw they were until he spent time with Kendall.

Until he craved *more* with Kendall. More sex. More conversations. More time. Just *more*.

"What do you say we head back to the ship?" She gave a slow smile. "This really hot guy asked me on a date, and I want plenty of time to get ready for it."

"Don't have to ask me twice."

CHAPTER 11

Kendall resented every minute she spent getting ready. She still couldn't believe she'd gone for it earlier today with Alex, that she'd told him she didn't want this to end. On the return trip to the ship, he'd held her hand and kept the conversation light as they exchanged anecdotes from their respective childhoods. Neither one of them had brought up the harsh realities about what might happen once this trip was over.

She didn't care. She refused to let something as dreary as distance threaten her happy moment. Grace was right. With all the technology at their disposal, they could see each other daily if they wanted to. No, that didn't substitute an in-person relationship—or sex—but it meant their living in different states wasn't a deal breaker.

Everything else would work itself out one way or another.

She smoothed her hand down one of the two nice dresses she'd packed for this trip. She'd bought it for the corporate manager's wedding a few years ago and had never worn it again. At the time, she'd felt like a fraud in the deep purple dress that skimmed her body from her breasts to her thighs before flaring out in a mermaid style. Now, knowing she'd see Alex in a little over an hour, she felt unstoppable.

She finished with her hair and quickly did her makeup. It was too warm to do anything too intense there, but she still went with a killer red lipstick that she'd bought when she aspired to be a bolder version of herself. At the time, it felt an impossible task to work up the courage to paint her lips *that* shade of red.

Tonight, she didn't hesitate to use it.

She stepped into the hallway feeling ten feet tall. The sensation only grew when she caught sight of Alex walking toward her. He wore a pair of slacks and a button-down gray shirt. He missed a step and his gaze narrowed on her in a way that made her feel like she was the only other person in the world. He stopped in front of her and grinned. "Hey."

"Hey."

"You look amazing."

"Thank you." She couldn't stop herself from reaching out and taking his hand. "You look pretty good yourself."

"I aim to please." He slipped her hand into the crook of his arm and turned them to head away from her room. They held an easy silence as they made their way to dinner. It wasn't until they were seated that Alex scooted his chair closer to hers. There might as well not have been other people at their table for how he acted, and she couldn't help doing the same.

"I have to tell you something." She leaned in and lowered her voice. "I think your friend is hooking up with *my* friend, Benjamin."

"Benjamin," Alex repeated. He suddenly smiled, wide and happy. "Well, look at that. Good for him." She must have looked confused, because he lowered his voice and explained. "Lucas doesn't date a lot of guys, so I'm glad he's getting out of his way on this trip."

"You two are really good friends, huh?"

"Yeah." Alex settled back into his chair. "We've known each other a long time. Both played football, but it was Pop who kind of created this safe space." His mouth twisted. "He had a habit of picking up strays, and Lucas had his own reasons for wanting a place he could be himself fully."

Every conversation they had continued to flesh out the picture of his life. She fiddled with her fork. "It's hard when they leave us, isn't it?"

Alex tensed, and seemed to force himself to relax. "Yeah. Though Pop is still alive, enjoying the hell out of his retirement in Mexico."

She almost asked how he felt about that, if he considered it an abandonment akin to his parents, but bit the question back at last moment. If he wanted to talk about that, she was more than happy to do so, but it was pure selfishness to ask him to crack himself open for her. Instead, she said, "Retirement sounds like a dream right now."

"Your job that bad?"

Kendall started to give her usual response that it wasn't *that* bad. She gave herself a shake. "The company has three hotels in the city and corporate likes to have their hands in everything whether they're qualified to make those calls or not. It's not so terrible all the time, but they continually pass me over for a promotion when they invariably run the most recent sales manager off. I have a lot of ideas for what could really elevate our hotels and set us apart, but while they're okay with me carrying the bulk of the sales responsibilities, they don't actually care what I have to say." It was the first time she'd spoken that truth aloud. Kendall put a brave face on for her sisters and her friends. She was living the dream in New York in a job that she mostly loved. What right did she have to complain about the things that didn't go well?

"What will you do if they pass you over again?"

Trust Alex to get right to the heart of it. She gave a helpless shrug. "I don't know. I don't really have a backup plan at this point, and the hotel will suffer without me. I'd hate to see the rest of the staff punished because I didn't get what I want."

He watched her with those blue eyes that always seemed to see too much. "Do you always make decisions based on how it will affect other people, even at the expense of yourself?"

She started to say that it wasn't at her expense, but Kendall couldn't lie in this moment. Not to herself and not to him. "Pretty much." She cleared her throat. "You know what it's like to have a grandparent take over raising you. They've already done the work raising a child to adulthood. Now they have to do it again, and even though my grandmother was strong and took over without missing a step, I couldn't help feeling like I was unwanted." She held up a hand. "Grams never, ever, made me feel that way. She's probably turning over in her grave right now to hear me say it, but I can't help the way I felt."

Alex gave a tight smile. "I hear you on the unwanted feeling, but we dealt with it in very different ways."

He acted out. She folded herself up until she fit perfectly within the boundaries of other people's expectations. "Yeah, I guess we did." She ran her hand down his arm. "Maybe we can learn from each other?"

"Maybe." Something in his tone made her wonder if it wasn't better to change the subject. They might be all up in their feelings right now over each other, but if his wounds from the past were anything like hers, they ran plenty deep.

She didn't want to trample all over them in her effort to get closer to him.

Kendall turned the conversation to lighter topics as they ate, and Alex let her do it. It didn't take long for the tension to fade from his shoulders and for him to be laughing. As the last of their meal was cleared away, she leaned back in her chair and smiled at him. "This has been really, really nice."

"It has, hasn't it?" His smile turned wicked. "Want to get out of here?"

"I thought you'd never ask."

* * *

ALEX PLANNED on taking Kendall back to his cabin, but she led him up to the deck. At his questioning look, she gave him a bright smile. "The sky seems so much bigger down here than it is in the city. I want to soak it in."

"Pop has a thing for falling stars. He's a superstitious old bastard." He chuckled. "When he was still in town, he'd drag me—and sometimes Lucas out of town to watch meteor showers. Made a whole lot of wishes on those nights."

Kendall didn't ask what he'd wished for, and he appreciated it. Maybe that was why he told her something he'd never told another person to date. "I used to wish for a big family. Pop is the best man I'll ever know, but at the end of the day he's only one man. I had friends with a bunch of siblings or cousins or whatever the fuck, and I craved that kind of safe chaos more than I ever wanted to admit."

She looked up at the stars, her smile soft and sweet. "Maybe you'll have it someday. The big happily messy family."

"Maybe." He'd given up that dream a long time ago, but standing here with Kendall, he could almost allow himself to wish for it again.

"I have a confession." Kendall stepped to the railing at the edge of the deck, still studying the sky. "I've never wished on a star."

"*What?*"

"I put away a lot of things when my parents died, and that childhood sense of magic was one of them. How can wishes come true when the only thing I wanted with all my heart, wished with all my soul, was that they were okay?"

God, his chest ached for her remembered pain. Alex stepped up behind her and folded his body around hers, offering her comfort the only way he knew how. Not with words. He was no good at that shit. But with touch. He held her close and waited for her to keep talking.

"I think I'd like to start now," she whispered. "How can I refuse to believe in magic when this sequence of events put you in my life? It's too big to be a simple coincidence." She laughed a little. "Sorry if that's too heavy."

"It's not." He felt the same way. Like they had spent their whole lives flying through space to reach this one point of impact. Alex didn't know if he really believed in destiny, but he wasn't going to question whatever force had set them on a collision course.

She shivered in his arms. Alex couldn't help shifting her hair off the back of her neck and pressing a kiss there. He meant it to be... Fuck, he didn't even know. But Kendall threw that plan out the window when she arched back against him. "Touch me," she breathed.

As if he'd deny her anything.

Alex ran his hands up her sides and back down again, enjoying the way she twisted against him, obviously trying to guide his touch. He finally relented and cupped her breasts through her dress and then pressing the heel of his hand against her clit. It wasn't enough. He knew that even before her breath escaped her in a sob.

"Unzip my dress."

He shot a look around them, but they'd wandered down the side of the deck and there was no one nearby. Even if someone *did* see them, his body should more than hide Kendall's. He moved back just enough to drag down the ridiculously tiny zipper. Her dress sagged away from her body and he slipped his hands beneath it to cup her bare breasts. She was so fucking perfect it blew his mind. Physically, yes, but her unfurling confidence drew him like a moth to flames. He just hoped he wouldn't be burned up in his desire to get closer. Endlessly closer.

Alex skimmed his hand down her stomach and paused. "Sweetheart."

"Mmmm?"

"Do you *ever* wear panties?"

Kendall laughed, low and wicked. "Not since meeting you."

He cupped her pussy, loving the way she arched back against him, seeking his cock even as he pushed two fingers into her. The dress kept her from spreading her legs, though she tried. He kissed her neck again, lingering there. "Better?" he murmured against her skin. Giving this woman exactly what she asked for had become his kink. He couldn't get enough of it. He couldn't get enough of *her*.

"Yes. No." She shivered in his arms. "Alex..." Kendall pushed back against his body harder and then she shoved her dress down until it was just past her hips, baring herself to him. "I need you," she whispered.

Fuck.

He fumbled in his pocket with his free hand, finally coming up with the condom he'd tucked there earlier on a whim. He should have known he'd end up using it. Kendall liked fucking in public too much to risk going without, which was something he should have learned by now. He was forced to release her to rip open the foil and roll it onto his cock. "You're going to kill me."

"You keep saying that." She moaned as he pressed his hand flat against her back, bending her forward a little as he guided his cock into her pussy.

"I keep meaning it," he gritted out. Alex leaned forward to finger her clit with one hand and grip the railing with the other. "Eyes up, sweetheart. You're going to miss a shooting star if you get distracted."

"Can't have... that."

He sheathed himself in her completely and held still has he worked her clit. "No, we really can't." He nipped her shoulder. "You're going to get me arrested for public indecency."

"Worth it." She thrust back against him, but he held her too tightly for her to be able to do more than writhe on his cock. "Oh god, that feels good."

"Only for you, sweetheart. I would only lose my head like this for you." He pulled out a little more and pushed back into her. "You start asking me for shit, begging for my cock, and I can't do anything but give it to you exactly how you want it."

"Harder. Deeper. Fuck me, Alex. Right here, beneath the stars."

"*Christ.*" He moved back and grabbed her hips. And then he did exactly as she commanded, fucking her in deep, harsh strokes. He couldn't shield her body like this, couldn't cover her as he drove into her again and again. And that only seemed to make Kendall hotter. She let go of her dress and held onto the railing, her mostly naked body slamming back onto him with each thrust. Fucking him as intensely as he fucked her. Meeting him stroke for stroke. Driving him higher.

He slapped her ass and then took a handful, squeezing the

same spot. "That's right, greedy girl. Take my cock. Take every single fucking inch."

"Yes!"

He caught movement out of the corner of his eye and didn't hesitate. Alex stepped close to her, pinning her between him in the railing and yanking her dress up as much as he could even as he leaned down to let the sides of his jacket drape over her. Kendall froze as two drunk guys walked toward them. They weren't moving quickly, though, and Alex cursed himself for letting them get into this situation. He wanted to give her everything she wanted, but not at expense to her. If this upset her…

But Kendall surprised him. She took his hand that wasn't holding her dress up and tugged it down to slid between the fabric and her body. To stroke her clit while two drunk idiots stumbled by not ten feet away.

Alex didn't know if he wanted to kill her…or propose on the spot.

All he knew was that his woman had very clearly given an order, and he had a promise to keep. He circled her clit and spoke softly in her ear. "Dirty girl. You want to come where they can see you, don't you?"

"Yes," she breathed. "Is that wrong?"

"Nothing we do together is wrong, sweetheart." He applied just the kind of pressure he'd learned that she craved and kept up the rhythm designed to send her over the edge. She was already so fucking primed, she shook with the effort it took to keep still.

The men passed behind them, so close that Alex could have reached out and touched them. If they weren't drunk off their asses, they might have noticed that he was balls deep in Kendall right now, but they were too busy arguing about the most recent superhero movie. They kept going, and he kept winding Kendall tighter and tighter.

"*Alex.*" She whimpered.

He knew what she needed without her saying it this time. He pulled her hands to her dress to take over and then covered her mouth with his hand. Just like that, Kendall was coming, her body shaking and her moan vibrating against his palm.

He barely waited for the idiots to turn the corner before he pulled out of her and yanked her dress into place. He forced himself to slow down so he didn't break the zipper, but only barely. By the time Kendall turned around, he had his cock shoved back in his pants.

"You didn't come."

"No, I didn't." He grabbed her hand and started for the elevators. "I want you in a bed, sweetheart. Now."

CHAPTER 12

*E*very time Kendall thought she couldn't possibly want Alex more, she went and proved herself wrong. She couldn't believe what they'd done on the deck, and as they slammed into his cabin, she was already aching for him again. She wrestled herself out of her dress as he yanked off his clothes.

They paused, both naked and breathing hard, and stared at each other.

Kendall burst out laughing. "Apparently we missed the memo that we're supposed to be smooth and sophisticated and undress each other in a seductive way."

"Save that shit for the movies." He scooped her up and dropped them both onto the bed. Kendall shrieked, and he touched her stomach. "You ticklish?"

She grabbed his wrist. "The last guy who decided to find out got kicked in his face for his trouble. Accidentally, of course."

Alex laughed. "No tickling then."

"Thank you." She took his face in her hands and kissed him deeply. "Seriously, *thank you*. For this entire week. It's been better than I could have dreamed even when I thought it was going to go according to plan. I never could have planned on you."

"I couldn't have planned on you either, sweetheart." He pressed kisses along her jawline and down her neck. "My little exhibitionist."

"I never knew." She laced her fingers through his hair as he moved to her breasts. "I mean, I knew what turned me on in the books I read, but I never realized it could be like that in real life." Except... was this real life? It didn't feel like it with this gorgeous man kissing his way down her body, his intentions clear. This man who gave her anything she asked for as long as she put voice to the words.

This man she might be falling in love with, though it was too soon by any measurement of time. Four days to fall in love with a complete stranger? If one of her friends claimed as much, she'd have sat them down for a serious talk about endorphins and pheromones and fantasy having nothing to do with reality.

But now that it was happening to her? She couldn't deny how *real* it felt.

Alex settled between her thighs and went after her pussy as if he hadn't had his mouth all over her a few short hours ago. She'd never felt sexier than she did in these moments, when he touched her or looked at her or spoke to her as if she was this gift he was certain he didn't deserve. Alex was wrong on that count. If there was anyone who didn't deserve this, it was her. What had she done to earn it? Show up in the right time and right place?

Her thoughts dissipated as Alex fucked her with his tongue. Every muscle in Kendall's body went hot and molten. "That feels so freaking good." She reached down and laced her fingers through his hair, clinging to him as she rode his face. Alex's grip on her thighs tightened and he picked up his pace, matching her rising hips. As if he was as turned on by doing this as she was.

She never would have even *thought* to go there with another guy, to be a little rough as she guided him exactly where she wanted him. But Alex wasn't another guy, and what they had was special. Maybe it was how he demanded open communication. Maybe it was just *him*. She didn't know. In the end, all the mattered was that she didn't want it to stop.

Her body tightened as her orgasm drew near. It would be the easiest thing in the world to relax into it like she had every time in the past. To simply take it as he offered.

Kendall wanted more.

"Come here." She tugged on his hair. "I want you inside me when I come."

Alex sucked on her clit hard and then kissed his way up her body. "How do you want it, sweetheart?"

Did he realize how effectively he undid her every time he asked that question? Because he truly wanted to know, truly wanted to give it to her. She gave him a quick kiss. "I want to try..." So many things. Countless possibilities she'd only fantasized about. He'd already knocked a few off the list. "Reverse cowgirl."

"Don't have to tell me twice." He moved to his back and grabbed a condom.

"Let me." Kendall snagged it and met his gaze as she ripped it open. "I've never done this before."

Alex blinked. "Why not?"

It was such a dude thing to ask, she laughed. "Because I was never able to get out of my head enough to think I'd actually enjoy it." She rolled the condom down his cock slowly. "I want it with you. I want you to watch me."

"My little exhibitionist." He sat up and kissed her hard.

Kendall gave him a little push and moved to straddle him

facing away. It took a little maneuvering to slide onto his cock, but the new angle was an immediate reward. "*Oh.*"

He ran his hands down her hips and squeezed her ass. "Ride me. Take what you need."

She leaned forward and braced her hands on his thighs. Alex's muffled curse only drove her wilder. She rode his cock, chasing her pleasure, driven by the way he touched and stroked her. As if she was the most precious thing he'd ever possessed. Kendall had never felt sexier than she did in that moment, and the sensation pushed her over the edge. She ground down on him as she came.

Alex barely waited for her to finish before he rolled them. He urged her hips up and then he was slamming into her, driving as deep as he could. "Can't... get...enough."

"More." She fisted her hands in the comforter. "Harder."

"Fuck." He gave a strangled laugh. And then he did as she commanded, fucking her until the slap of flesh against flesh filled the room. Her toes curled and then he was coming, his fingers digging hard into her hips and his curses filling her ears.

Alex collapsed next to her. "Give me a second." He rolled out of bed and went to dispose of the condom in the bathroom. Then he came back and laid down next to her, pulling her into his arms. "Whew."

"Whew," she repeated. She couldn't stop grinning. "That about sums it up."

"I don't care what you say, Kendall Barnes. You're a straight up wild child." He stroked his hand over her hair and down her back.

She smiled harder and pressed a kiss to his chest. "When I'm with you, I actually feel like one. Thank you."

"You have nothing to thank me for, sweetheart. It's all you."

In that moment, she actually believed him.

* * *

FOR THE THIRD TIME, Alex woke up with Kendall wrapped around him. He smiled even before he opened his eyes. Truth be told, he thought he'd smiled more in the last couple days than in the last few months. It was just so fucking easy with her.

He should be afraid of that. He knew it deep down where part of him never quite let go of the pain of his parents leaving. Caring too deeply about other people meant handing them your heart and hoping they didn't take it with them when they invariably called it quits.

Kendall had more of his heart than he dared admit.

He opened his eyes and looked down at her. She was so fucking cute. Cute and sexy and funny and wicked smart. Too good for him, no doubt about it, but she didn't seem to care. She didn't want this to end any more than he did. He didn't know what a future with her might look like, but he wasn't ready to be done. Not by a long shot.

She shifted without opening her eyes and scrunched up her nose. "You're watching me sleep."

"Guilty."

"That's very creepy of you."

He laughed and smoothed a hand down her back. "Correction—it's only very creepy of me if I snuck into your room without an invitation and *then* watched you sleep. You're in my room, sweetheart. It's fair game."

"I don't remember reading that in the rules." She stretched, creating some distance between them. "I need to brush my teeth."

"By all means." He waited for her to use the bathroom and then took his turn. Soon enough, they were back in his bed, and he couldn't shake how *nice* this was. This closeness and ease between them. It wasn't just sex, no matter what they both might fear. "Do you want to do an excursion today?"

She made a face. "I suppose we should, right?"

He didn't want to. He just wanted to stay here, wrapped up in her until they were forced out of the room by the end of the trip. Even now, even knowing they both wanted more, he couldn't help seeing a clock ticking down the minutes until the time when the cruise ended and they had to say goodbye. It might not be forever, but life got in the way more often than it helped out.

Alex sat up. "What are you doing for Memorial Day?"

"For... Memorial Day?"

"Yeah."

Kendall blinked. "I don't have plans. Probably work?"

"Take the three-day weekend and come down to Dawson's Creek. I'll show you around, and we can make the most of it." He hesitated when she just kept watching him. "You don't have to. I know we said what we said, but if this is just a vacation hookup for you, then no pressure."

She reached out and pressed her fingers to his lips, stilling his words. "It's not just a vacation fling for me, Alex. I'm just surprised. It makes it so much more real to make plans for later, you know?"

"I know," he spoke against her fingertips. "Like I said—"

"I'll book tickets the second I get back to New York."

Something unclenched in his chest and he smiled. "Okay. Cool. Yeah, okay."

She answered his smile with one of her own. "Then you'll have to come up to New York for Fourth of July. Or maybe we can meet somewhere in the middle."

"Deal." This was happening. It was really happening. He could barely believe it. Alex flopped back onto his pillow, taking Kendall with him. "I think you're right. We should do an excursion today. They had a shit ton of options."

"I'm thinking the private beach." She gave a wicked smile. "There's a lighthouse."

Alex fought to keep his expression even despite wanting to grin right back. "Sweetheart, are you about to tell me that you want to fuck in a lighthouse?"

"I mean... I wouldn't be opposed to the idea."

Alex couldn't hold it together any longer. He laughed and pressed a kiss to her temple. "We'll see what we can come up with."

"Mmm." She ran her hand down his chest. "Speaking of coming up..."

He rolled her onto her back and settled between her thighs. "You're insatiable."

"It's your fault." She kissed his jaw, his neck, his shoulder. "I've never been like this until I met you."

He managed to remember himself enough to back up and grab one of the condoms in the bowl on the nightstand. He rolled it over his cock and eased himself into Kendall. She pulled him closer, tugging his face down to hers and claimed his mouth. They moved together as one, neither rushing, as if she relished this slow, intimate moment just as much as he did. He never wanted it to end.

He never wanted any of this to end.

Kendall writhed around him as she orgasms, and Alex didn't resist the desire to follow her over the edge. He came with her name on his tongue and fuck if that moment didn't feel downright spiritual.

Right up until someone pounded on the door.

He lifted his head. "What?"

"Is Kendall Barnes in there?"

Alex frowned. He didn't recognize the voice. "Yeah. One second." He climbed off the bed, disposed of the condom, and yanked on a pair of shorts. Kendall held up her dress, but he tossed her one of his shirts. "Easier."

"Thank you." She pulled it over her head and it covered enough to work.

He opened the door and frowned at the white guy in a cruise employee uniform standing there. "What's up?"

But the guy wasn't looking at him. He peered around Alex to Kendall. "Ms. Barnes? I'm going to need you to come with me."

Her eyes went wide. "Is everything okay?"

"I'm going to need you to come with me," he repeated.

Oh shit. No way was this anything but bad news. Alex held up a hand. "Give us a second to get some clothes on. Does she have time to go to her cabin first?"

The guy looked away, visibly uncomfortable. "It'd be best if she didn't."

Kendall went pale. "Is it my friends? Did something happen?"

Alex could see that the guy was about to give another vague answer that wouldn't do a damn thing but stress her out more, so he cut in. "Let's find you some shorts with ties and we'll get some answers." He hesitated. "Unless you don't want me to come with you."

"I do." She accepted the shorts he handed her and pulled them on, barely pausing to cinch the waist in tight. He had a spare pair of flip-flops stuff in his suitcase, so he handed her those as well. For his part, Alex finished getting dressed in record time.

He followed Kendall to the door. "Let's go."

a thousand and one horrible scenarios went through Kendall's mind as she and Alex followed the cruise employee to a private room. He passed them off to a Latino woman in clothing that spoke of management. She didn't blink at Kendall's clothing or at Alex's presence at her back. "Ms. Barnes?"

"Yes, that's me." She twisted the hem of her shirt—of Alex's shirt—between her hands. "What's going on? Did something happen to one of my friends?"

"As far as I know, everyone who accompanied you on this trip is fine." She hesitated. "But there seems to be a family emergency." She passed over a quickly scrawled note that was obviously written by someone taking a message.

Ethan in hospital. It looks bad. Gretchen is a wreck. Get your ass home.
- Marley

"I have to go." She hadn't realized she spoke aloud until Alex tensed at her back. She couldn't focus on him, though, not with her plans unfurling before her. She met the manager's gaze. "I'm going to need to book a flight from the island."

"We can help arrange that." Another hesitation, the woman obviously didn't want to be a dick, but that didn't stop her from saying, "Of course, we cannot facilitate a refund at this juncture."

As if Kendall cared the least bit about that. She waved the woman's words away. "I'm not concerned about it. I'm going to pack."

"Of course. I'll send one of our people to collect you and help you book the flight."

Every moment she stood there, she wasted time. "Thanks." She turned and nearly ran into Alex. For a second, she'd actually forgotten he was in the room. She started to say—she didn't know what. It didn't matter in the end. Alex shifted back to let her pass and fell into step behind her as she hurried back to her cabin. She barely glanced at him as she started shoving clothing into her suitcase.

"Kendall."

She didn't look up. "I'm sorry, but I have to go."

"Kendall, look at me."

If she stopped, she'd start thinking about the implications of Gretchen's husband in the hospital, about how serious it must be in order to be called home, about what it meant that *Marley* knew before she did and was the one to contact her instead of Gretchen. Bad, bad, bad. No matter which way she looked at it, it was bad.

She turned and nearly ran into Alex. Again. "I have to pack."

"Kendall." The snap in his voice slowed her down long enough to look at him. She expected some kind of judgment or anger. He just looked worried. "What do you need from me?"

"I need to go," she repeated. "I... I'll call you." She would.

Once she knew what she was dealing with and could think straight.

Alex looked at her for a long moment and finally nodded. "Okay, sweetheart. Like I said—whatever you need." He walked to her nightstand and scrawled a number there. "I'll be home the day the ship docks. If you need me before then, call anyways."

"Okay," she whispered, already knowing she wouldn't.

Another of those long looks, as if he could already see her wavering on the future of them. "Talk to me, Kendall. I know this shit isn't about me, but you don't have to shoulder the burden alone."

Kendall didn't share burdens. It wasn't how she operated. She had to focus on her sister and the crisis requiring her presence, not the man standing in front of her. She stripped quickly out of his clothing and dressed in the first pair of shorts and top she found. "I don't know what I'm walking into, Alex. I just know my brother-in-law is in the hospital, and that it's serious or I wouldn't have had a call while I was on this trip. My little sister isn't even living in Oregon right now, so the fact that *she* is the one calling me in speaks volumes."

"I understand that." A hint of frustration slid into his tone, and she resented the hell out of it.

She shoved the rest of her clothes into her suitcase, not bothering to fold them. "What if it's a prolonged illness? What if I have to stay there for weeks and eat up the rest of my vacation time? I don't get more until the new year."

He crossed his arms over his chest. "What are you saying?"

She didn't know. She couldn't *think*. "I'm saying that I can't make promises to you, and it's not fair to ask you to wait for me. Nine months before I can see you again? Or nine months where you're the one who has to fly to me? This is the first vacation you've taken in years. You're not going to leave your beloved bar more than absolutely necessary, and we both know this is hardly *necessary*."

"So when you say you'll call me, what you're really saying is not to wait by the phone because this shit isn't going to happen."

"I really don't want to do this now."

He didn't move. "We don't dock for another twenty minutes. You can't do fuck all until then."

Maybe not, but it would still feel good to move. "I'm sorry. I didn't want to leave it like this."

"Maybe not, but you're sure as shit doing it." He took a slow step back. "It's fine, Kendall. I hear you loud and clear. Good luck with your family. I truly hope your brother-in-law is okay." He picked up his clothing that she'd discarded and walked out the door of her cabin, letting it close softly behind him.

Kendall couldn't breathe past the pounding of her heart. Every atom in her body wanted to chase Alex down and beg him to understand where she was coming from. She was worried and scared and didn't know what kind of situation she would walk into when she got back to Oregon. She wasn't in the same position to make promises the same way she had been last night.

She forcibly put the thought of Alex from her mind. He didn't need her. Her sister did. In the end, that was what it came down to.

She tried to knock on her friends' cabin doors, but either they were sleeping too hard or none of them were in their rooms. Another time, that thought would make her happy, the realization that they were all enjoying their vacation despite the setbacks. Now all she felt was frustration that she didn't know where to find them. Kendall scrawled out a quick note explaining what had happened and where she'd gone and pushed it under Grace's door.

Then there was nothing else to do, Kendall headed for the manager's office to figure out how she'd get on a flight out of Nassau to Oregon. Once she was there, she'd figure out her next steps. Maybe it wasn't as bad as it seemed.

Kendall desperately hoped it wasn't as bad as it seemed.

* * *

It took Kendall two days to get to Oregon. She ended up stuck in the Dallas airport and then flown into Portland and had to rent a car to drive up the coast to where Ruby Creek was nestled. Through it all, the only information Marley gave her was that it was bad and to hurry.

She hurried.

She found her sisters in the hallway of the hospital, huddled together and talking in low voices. Gretchen looked up first and, Kendall knew in that moment that Ethan wouldn't make it. Her sister didn't look like herself. Pain was written over every inch of her face, her shoulders were stooped, and there was a numbness in her blue eyes that reached out and kicked Kendall right in the teeth.

Gretchen didn't even smile. "You're here."

"I'm here." She glanced at Marley, their little sister, the one who always looked like sunshine and rainbows. Her blond hair was pulled back into a simple ponytail and she had on jeans and a plain white T-shirt. More indicators of the severity of the situation, as if Kendall needed them. "What do you need?"

"We were just going to go home for a little while to rest."

Gretchen shook her head. "I'm fine."

"You are *not* fine." Marley turned a pleading look at

Kendall, and that was all she needed to snap out of her shock and into planning mode.

She stepped up and took her sister's elbow. "Let's get showered and eat something and we can come right back here. You have to take care of yourself, Gretchen." Before her older sister could protest, she had guided them downstairs to the front door and out into the parking lot.

An hour later, she closed the door on her sleeping sister, her heart breaking at the way Gretchen curled around what was obviously Ethan's pillow. Just as she'd hoped, exhaustion caught up with her sister the second she stopped moving. It wouldn't slow her down for long—not knowing Gretchen—but it would help.

Kendall went and found Marley in the kitchen. "Tell me."

"He had a stroke."

"A *stroke?* Ethan's barely thirty-five."

Marley transferred scoop after scoop of coffee into the filter. "Yeah, I know. Kendall... It's bad. Really bad. Like he isn't going to make it bad." She took a deep breath. "And Gretchen is pregnant."

"*What?*" She twisted to look back at the room where she'd left her sister. "I didn't know."

"No one knew. They had a miscarriage a few years ago and so they weren't going to tell anyone until she had her first ultrasound." Marley gave a sad smile. "I only know now because she passed out and had to tell me to avoid me dragging her to a doctor, too."

Marley had been here for *days* holding down the fort. Kendall pulled her sister into a tight hug. "You've done a great job, Marley."

"There's more."

How could there possibly be more? She braced herself. "Okay."

Marley didn't release her. "She and Ethan scraped up

everything they had to secure a loan. They bought Mom and Dad's old restaurant. Construction is supposed to start the week after next." She hesitated. "They put a lien on their house to do it."

Oh, Gretchen. "We'll figure it out.

"I'm scared for her."

"Me too." She gave her sister a last squeeze and stepped back. "I'm here now. You don't have to do this alone."

It was only later, when she finally got her bags into her old room to unpack, that she had a moment to mourn the loss of Alex. Because it was a loss. From what she'd been able to glean from the doctors, the chance of Ethan waking up decreased with every hour. The stroke had created a pressure in his brain that they weren't able to release.

Gretchen was going to be a widow. A pregnant widow. A pregnant widow who had just risked everything to secure a loan to buy the old restaurant that had belonged to their parents once upon a time.

Kendall had thought she had a strong path in life. She'd worked hard in high school, gotten into the college she wanted, graduated with as little student debt as she could manage, settled into a job that was supposed to be her forever career.

It all felt like so much bullshit now.

She called the hotel, her heart in her throat. "Please put me through to Valerie." She and the current general manager didn't often see eye to eye, but surely they would on this. Family was everything.

A few seconds later, Valerie answered with a brisk, "Hello?"

"Hi Valerie. It's Kendall."

"Must not be enjoying your vacation that much if you're calling work in the middle of it."

She closed her eyes and strove for patience. "I was called

away from the vacation because of a family emergency. That's actually why I'm calling now. I need more time."

"No."

She actually took the phone from her ear and looked at it, sure she'd heard wrong. "What?"

"We can't spare you. I haven't had a chance to fill the sales manager position, so we need you here."

Kendall could feel her patience slipping through her fingers, but she tried to keep her tone bright. "Valerie, I sent you a short list of the applicants." Including hers. There was no reason Valerie shouldn't have scheduled interviews for this week, even if she wasn't going to give Kendall the job.

"I saw that you put yours in. Again." The bite disappeared from Valerie's tone. "If you take time like this, it's going to negatively affect your career, Kendall. I can't have a sales manager who disappears for... how long are you requesting?"

"I don't know."

"You don't know." Valerie echoed. "You must know I can't approve that."

She guessed she did. "You were never going to give me that position, were you?"

"You're very good where you're at. I have to manage my assets accordingly."

That answered that, didn't it? She looked back over all the wasted years of breaking herself in that job to prove her worth. For what? So her boss could keep her pigeon-holed and then not even have the empathy to allow her to take time off for this family emergency? Was *that* really the company she'd sacrificed so much for?

In the end, there was no choice at all. A weight she'd been carrying for far too long fell away and she stood straighter. "I quit."

"Excuse me?"

"I. Quit. Expect my emailed resignation in the morning." She hung up and sank onto the bed. Holy crap, she'd done it. There was no safety net. No backup plan. She'd just have to make it work.

She reached for her phone, driven by the urge to call Alex and tell him...

And stopped.

She'd just quit her job. Her rent was paid through the next two months, but she'd have to get back to New York and figure out what to do with it since she didn't have an income any longer. The very last thing she'd expected when she rushed to her sisters' sides was that she'd be... moving back to Ruby Creek. That's what was happening. No point in side-stepping it. Gretchen needed her, and there wasn't a timeline on when that would stop. It would take a miracle for Ethan to recover, and even then he wouldn't be able to be the partner on this renovation project like they'd planned. A renovation project that would overlap with her sister's pregnancy and the birth of her new baby.

Kendall pressed her hands to her chest, the echoes of Gretchen's pain nearly sending her into a fetal position. She couldn't put a timeline on her older sister finding her feet again. She *wouldn't*. Gretchen had been such a force of nature, a steady point to guide her life. No, her path had never been Kendall's, but her presence and confidence had grounded Kendall when she needed it time and time again.

Realistically, she was looking at years in Ruby Creek. Once the restaurant was done, it would have to be *opened* and run.

She might never leave this town again.

It was one thing to try for a long-distance relationship when she had a job and an income and a hell of a lot of vacation days saved up. In the course of a few hours, her entire life had been derailed. She couldn't ask Alex to shoulder the burden of flying to see her—or paying for her flights to him. If they were both occupied with running businesses…

No time.

There was simply no time.

She set her phone down and nudged it away. It hurt so much to think of never seeing him again, but it was the right choice for both of them. It had to be. Better to let them mourn the idea of what could have been now, rather than drag it out and sink emotions and money and time into something that was destined to fail.

No matter how much it hurt now to contemplate never seeing him again.

CHAPTER 14

*I*t took two weeks for Alex to fully give up hope of hearing from Kendall. Two weeks of jumping every time his phone rang, quickly followed by sour disappointment. Two weeks of trying to convince himself that maybe his worst fears were wrong.

He prowled around Pop's, aggressively cleaning until everything shone, going over the menu for the specials over the next month, reconfiguring his filing system. Doing everything in his power to stay busy so he didn't have to think too hard about what he'd lost. *Who* he'd lost.

Kendall.

It shouldn't be possible to have his heart broken after less than a week with a person, but he couldn't deny the truth ticking beat by jagged beat in his chest. Lust didn't hurt like this. It didn't leave him feeling bruised and battered and still wanting to see her more than anything else in the world. It didn't tip his entire life upside down and shake it for all it was worth until he questioned the priorities and rules he'd lived by for a decade.

Only love did that.

He didn't look up as someone walked through the door to his office. "I'm busy."

"Really? Because it looks like you're moping."

The gravely voice was so unexpected, it took Alex a few moments to process it. He looked up and, sure enough, it was Pop standing there in his office. He stood a little straighter than the last time Alex had seen him, his skin browner from spending a lot of time in the sun, and he wore a Hawaiian shirt similar to the ones he'd insisted Alex don for the cruise.

Alex blinked again, but the old man didn't disappear. "What are you doing here?"

"I heard you got your head turned by a woman on the cruise and you've been unbearable ever since." Pop walked into the office and shut the door behind him. "I'm here to save you from yourself."

"I don't need saving."

"That's bullshit and you know it." Pop sank into the chair across the desk from him. "I like what you've done with the place."

The change in subject about gave him whiplash. "We get a lot less bar fights now."

"Suppose it was time for a change." Pop gave a rough smile. "Nostalgia only takes a person so far."

"Yeah, though I made sure to create a place for the regulars." He shifted, not totally comfortable with the close way Pop watched him. Historically, every time the old man did that, Alex ended up confessing whatever the fuck he'd been up to lately, despite his best efforts to keep silent. Even as he told himself to shut the hell up, he found himself speaking. "Just because I met a woman doesn't mean I need an intervention."

"Tell me about her."

It hurt to do it, but he did it anyway. "She was magic, Pop. If I'd imagined my perfect woman, she wouldn't come close to Kendall. We have a shit ton in common and our chemistry..." He trailed off. Some subjects just weren't for family. "It was unreal."

Pop studied him for a moment. "Lucas said she had to leave the cruise early. Some kind of family emergency."

Now Alex knew who to blame for this intervention. "Yeah."

"So what are you waiting for?"

Alex frowned. "What are you talking about?"

Pop leaned forward and spoke slowly as if talking to a child. "Go get your woman."

As if it was that easy. As if he hadn't actually considered doing exactly that before he discarded it. Alex had little left but his pride at this point. If people walked away from him, he didn't chase them, no matter how much their leaving hurt. Did his pride keep him warm at night? Fuck no. But at least he knew that he hadn't debased himself for someone who didn't give enough of a damn about him to stay. "When you chase down a woman who said she'd call and didn't, that's considered stalking and generally frowned upon."

Pop harrumphed. "Under normal circumstances, hell yeah. I would whoop your ass if I thought you were going after some woman who didn't want it."

"You don't know Kendall. You don't know that she *does* want it." Why was he even engaging in this argument? It didn't matter what Pop thought. He wasn't going after her. She hadn't texted, called, sent a carrier pigeon. Easy enough to read in between the lines, and that said she enjoyed their time together but it was finished. End of story.

Pop sat back. "Lucas said her brother-in-law died. Apparently it was a stroke or something like that." He narrowed his eyes. "And her older sister, the new widow, is pregnant."

The knowledge shuddered around Alex. He cleared his

throat. "Lucas seems to have a whole hell of a lot of information."

"Guess he's dating one of her friends. Nice boy from what I understand." Pop gave a brief smile. "But we're not talking about him. We're talking about you and your stubborn pride. Your woman needs you and you're sitting here, feeling sorry for yourself. I didn't raise you to be this selfish."

"*Selfish?*" Alex started to push to his feet and cut off the motion to slouch back in his chair. "It's not being selfish to prioritize the company *you* spent your entire adult life building to the successful business that it is. The pillar of the community, though they'd never call it that. Pop's is important. I'm needed here."

"Pop's is a bar," Pop said almost gently. "It's a building. Four walls and some shit inside. You've done good work, Alex. No one will say otherwise. But I never wanted you to end up like me—married to the place. You're too young for that shit, have too much living left to do."

"Pop's needs me." *It will never leave me.*

"Kendall needs you." Pop pushed slowly to his feet. "I'll be in town for a week or two. There's a flight out to Portland tonight if you decide to get over yourself before then." He stopped. "I'm proud of you, kid. I've *been* proud of you this whole time. It's not selfish to fight to find and hold onto happiness. Life is too short to do anything else." He turned and walked out of the office, leaving Alex staring after him.

He wanted to reject the words, to reject the knowledge of what Kendall was going through now. Easier to leave things black and white, cut and dried. She left, end of story.

Except... it wasn't the end of the story.

He scrubbed his hands over his face. Her brother-in-law hadn't survived. Her sister's perfect life was on fire. Kendall would be right there in the middle of it, taking care of everyone around her. Would she take care of herself in the process? Nope. Of course not. Not unless someone intervened, and they'd all be too focused on her older sister to worry about her, especially if she didn't show any outward signs of struggling.

It was sheer lunacy to go to her. She drew her line in the sand, life events influencing that or not. If he showed up without an invitation, she'd reject him right to his face instead of with her silence. Alex pressed the heel of his hand to his chest. It fucking *hurt* now, with a little thread of what-if hanging before him. He couldn't imagine what it would feel like to have that tiny possibility closed off.

Still wrapped in his thoughts, he headed out into the main room to check on things. Cherry worked behind the bar, all smiles for the customers though she could cut a man off at the knees if he stepped out of line. The tables scattered through the rest of the room were half filled, and his guy who was working part time as he went through college flitted between them, easily taking orders from memory and balancing the food and drinks when he delivered them. Everything ran like a well-oiled machine.

Normally, witnessing that was enough to warm Alex, to give him a deep sense of accomplishment. Yeah, he was still lonely, but he'd helped build this community and he took pride in that. Right now, all he felt was empty. The world didn't shine quite as brightly when Kendall wasn't in the room.

What the fuck was he doing? Was he really going to let her go just because she hadn't called him for help in the middle of a crisis? What the hell was *wrong* with him?

Alex strode behind the bar and waited for Cherry to finish pouring three shots and distributing them. She turned to him, one pierced eyebrow raised. "Yes, boss?"

"I'm going to be gone for a couple days. Maybe a week." He hoped. "Pop's in town if you need anything."

She rolled her eyes, but she smiled when she did it. "Don't you know by now that we can mostly handle things without you?"

"I'm beginning to see that."

"*Finally.*" She laughed and smacked his shoulder. "Get out of here. We have this covered. I'll call if I need anything."

He couldn't quite manage to make a joke about not burning the place down in his absence, but he gave a tight smile and left. A quick trip home to throw some stuff into an overnight bag and he was on his way to the airport. It wasn't until he was actually sitting in the plane that the reality of what he was doing rolled over him. In a few hours, he'd see Kendall again. He didn't know what that would look like, what would come of this. He didn't know anything, but he was going to try.

Pop was right—he'd never forgive himself if he didn't.

* * *

KENDALL HAD NEVER BEEN SO tired in her life. Between her and Marley, they'd managed to balance the tasks that came from seeing someone from death to burial. Going down the checklist she'd created felt morbid and reminded her of when her grandmother died, which dredged up more emotions she didn't have the capacity to deal with right now. They'd helped Gretchen pick a plot in the cemetery—one in the same area as Ethan's family going back generations—and the casket and the flowers and the pictures to use for the slideshow.

Through it all, Gretchen was just... numb. It wouldn't last. It *couldn't* last. But it was like her brain had shut down parts of itself to see her through this, like the trauma of losing Ethan was too much for her to truly comprehend. Kendall and Marley took turns coaxing her to eat and ensuring she drank enough water, because if left to her own devices, she forgot both.

If she lost this baby, too…

No. Kendall would *not* think about that.

She pulled on the same black dress she'd worn to Grams's funeral years ago and gave her hair one last cursory look. Her appearance didn't really matter, but she wouldn't give the town gossips any more fuel than they already had. They'd never bothered her much before—she was too much a perfectionist, even as a child, to give them ammunition for their whispers—but she'd be damned before she added to Gretchen's burden right now.

Marley waited for her downstairs. Her dress was shorter than it had a right to be and she had full makeup on her face, right down to the brilliant red lipstick. She gave a tight smile at Kendall's questioning look. "It's just backup, sis. I'll give those assholes something to talk about that isn't Gretchen."

She and Marley always had gone about things in different ways.

Gretchen met them there. She was too pale, the circles beneath her eyes standing out starkly. Her hair hung down to her shoulders in a lank wave and she moved as if she were decades older than her thirty-four years. "I'm ready."

It happened quickly after that. They arrived at the funeral home and went through the motions of watching the slideshow. Gretchen held it together during her speech, though she had to stop multiple times. Other people stood up and told stories about Ethan. How he'd helped them, laughed with them, been one of the pillars of this community. Kendall found Gretchen's hand and held it throughout, even as her sister's grip tightened and tightened, as if she could squeeze out her pain.

Then it was time to go to the grave site and do it all over again.

By the time they made it back to the house for the wake, Gretchen was leaning heavily on her. She guided her older sister to a chair in the back corner of the living room and went to check on the food they'd spent all yesterday preparing. The doorbell rang and then it was off to the races. She fell into a rhythm quickly. Greet. Accept condolences. Direct them to the food. Check in with Marley to make sure Gretchen was doing okay. Repeat. Over and over again, until the house felt like it would burst at the seams. By the time people got their fill of the wake and began leaving, she was weaving on her feet.

Just a little longer. Just hold it together a little longer.

The doorbell rang.

She closed her eyes and counted to five. She could do this one more time. Kendall took a deep breath that only shuddered a little and walked to the door. She pasted a smile on her face and opened it, but the words died on her lips when she found herself looking up at the man she never thought she'd see again. She blinked, but he didn't disappear. "Alex?"

"Hey, sweetheart." He glanced past her into the house, his expression carefully blank. "What can I do to help?"

With that single sentence, he dismantled anything she could have said. A simple offer of assistance she desperately needed. She swallowed past her suddenly dry throat. "Um, I need to put the food away."

"Show me."

She nodded shakily and led him into the house. Neither of them spoke as they started the process of putting the food away. Through it all, Kendall couldn't shake the feeling that this was a fever dream, that it couldn't possibly be real, that he couldn't be *here*, helping her in silence without demanding an explanation for her not calling once in the last couple weeks.

She put the last dish into the fridge. "Um, I need to check on my sister really quick."

"No rush." Alex slipped his hands into his pockets and studied her. "Want me to wait outside?"

"Maybe just wait here? There's beer in the fridge." She turned for the door and stopped. "And if Marley bursts in and starts interrogating you, just hold her off until I get back."

Alex raised his brows. "I've got it handled, sweetheart. Check on Gretchen."

She found Marley quietly closing the door to Gretchen's room. She gave a tired half-smile as Kendall walked up. "I convinced her to lay down for a few, but I think she was asleep before I left the room."

"Good. She needs it."

"Yeah." Marley glanced back at the closed door and her shoulders drooped. "We can't leave her."

"I know." Kendall nodded. "I already quit my job."

"I'm, uh, between jobs at the moment."

She laughed softly. "We'll talk about the future tomorrow, okay? Figure out a plan."

"You and your plans." Marley shook her head. "I need to get out of here for a little bit. Can you hold down the fort?"

She thought of the man waiting for her in the kitchen. "Yeah, I have things covered until you get back."

"You're the best." Marley squeezed her arm and then she was gone, snatching the keys and disappearing through the front door.

Kendall peeked into Gretchen's room, but as promised, she was out cold. Then there was nothing else to do but go back to the kitchen where Alex waited for her. He sat at the nook table, a beer bottle in front of him. When he saw her walk through the door, he pushed to his feet. "Hey."

"Hey." She worried her bottom lip, the events of the last

few days—few weeks—suddenly too much to hold. "I have questions about your showing up here, but... Would it be okay if you just held me for a minute?"

Alex's expression went soft. "Come here." She stepped into his arms and the second they closed around her, it was like her defenses crumbled. She clung to him and buried her face in his chest. Oh god, she was going to cry. Kendall started to push away, but Alex tightened his hug. "It's okay, sweetheart. I've got you. You don't have to be strong right now."

His words unraveled her. The tears came, hot and thick, and she sobbed until her throat felt just as ragged as her heart. Through it all, Alex held her close. He stroked her hair and murmured low words that wove a feeling of safety around them. For a second, she could almost believe that they'd all get through this, that it wasn't really the end of Gretchen's world, that Marley would be okay working through whatever was going on in her life, that Kendall hadn't made a mistake when she threw all her life plans away.

By the time she lifted her head and stepped back a little, she felt completely empty of grief for the first time since she walked into that hospital. It would be back. Of course it would be back. But in that moment, she actually felt better. "Thank you."

Alex brushed his thumbs across her cheekbones, wiping away the last of her tears. "Whatever you need, sweetheart. I'm here."

Selfish of her to consider *her* heart in the midst of all this loss, but she couldn't help it. "I never called."

"You had other things on your mind." He let his hands drop. "Do you want me to leave?"

Was that a trick question? Kendall let out a broken laugh. "No, Alex. I really, really don't want you to leave. I just... My sister needs me right now, and that isn't going to change in the next few months... or even years. I know I can't put my life entirely on hold to help her, but I also can't ask you to wait for me. It's not fair to you."

"Let me decide what's fair to me." He leaned back on the table, his blue eyes intense. "I'm not going to lie. It fucking hurt when you didn't call, even if I understand the reasoning behind it now. Every single time someone has walked away from me, I've let them do it because chasing after them..." He shook his head. "I have my pride, you know?"

"I know," she whispered.

"Except I don't when it comes to you. If I have to choose between my pride and you, it's you, Kendall. I know it's too soon for this shit, and I know you have more than enough to deal with without worrying about me, too, but what I'm trying to say is that I'll wait as long as it takes. I've never had a connection with another person the way I do with you, and I'm not willing to give it up just because things aren't lined up ideally right from the get-go." He shifted. "So what I'm asking you is if you're willing to try, too?"

She couldn't believe he was saying the things she hadn't dared hope for. She cleared her throat, and then had to do it again. "You'll end up resenting me."

"I won't." Alex shook his head. "We just need clear communication and some time."

A weightless feeling blossomed in her chest. "My sister bought a restaurant that needs to be completely renovated and then someone has to *run* it. That will take years, Alex. I don't know if I'll be leaving Ruby Creek anytime soon."

He shrugged. "Maybe things will go well and I'll end up here helping you with that." He threw it out so casually, as if it wasn't outside the realm of possibility. "We won't know until we try. That's all I'm asking, Kendall. Just *try* with me." He looked away and then back to her. "Unless you don't want to. If that's the case, then no hard feelings. You won't hear from me again." It cost him to get the words out. She could see that.

"Alex." Kendall stepped closer, looking up at him. "If you really mean it…"

"I do."

"Then *yes*. Yes, I want to try."

He wrapped his arms around her again, pulling her against his chest. "Thank fuck."

"I missed you. It doesn't make sense how much I missed you." She slid her arms around his neck. "I'm glad you're here."

He smiled. "I have about a week before I need to be back in Dawson's Creek. I'll do what I can to help in the meantime."

Her chest ached and felt melty, all at the same time. "I love you," she blurted. "I know it's too soon and that it's nuts but—"

Alex cut her off with a kiss. It wasn't a polite kiss, either. Not one designed to shut her up before she dug herself a deeper hole. No, he kissed her like he'd been waiting to hear those words his entire life and she'd just fulfilled his wish. When he finally lifted his head, she had to cling to him to keep her feet. "I love you, too. I don't care if it's too soon. It's the damn truth. This is a once in a lifetime kind of connection, and I'll do whatever it takes to ensure we have a happy future together, no matter how long I have to wait."

* * *

THANK you so much for reading Kendall and Alex's story! They're very special to me, and I hope you enjoyed reading them as much as I enjoyed writing them. If you did, please consider leaving a review!

If you're looking for something a little more *villainous* in your life, please consider checking out my series Wicked Villains. It begins with DESPERATE MEASURES, which is a dark erotic romance between Jafar and Jasmine that starts out with her bargaining and losing everything to him... including herself.

Looking for your next sexy read? You can pick up my MMF ménage THEIRS FOR THE NIGHT, my FREE novella that features an exiled prince, his bodyguard, and the bartender they can't quite manage to leave alone.

ABOUT THE AUTHOR

New York Times and USA TODAY bestselling author Katee Robert learned to tell her stories at her grandpa's knee. Her 2015 title, The Marriage Contract, was a RITA finalist, and RT Book Reviews named it 'a compulsively readable book with just the right amount of suspense and tension." When not writing sexy contemporary and romantic suspense, she spends her time playing imaginary games with her children, driving her husband batty with what-if questions, and planning for the inevitable zombie apocalypse.

www.kateerobert.com